Witch & Wizard

JAMES PATTERSON is one of the best-known and biggest-selling writers of all time. He is the author of two other popular series for young readers: Maximum Ride and Daniel X. This is as well as writing three of the top detective series around – the Alex Cross, Women's Murder Club and Detective Michael Bennett novels – and many other number one bestsellers including romance novels and stand-alone thrillers. He lives in Florida with his wife and son.

James is passionate about encouraging children to read. He was inspired by his own son, who was a reluctant reader, to write books specifically for young readers. James has also formed a partnership with the National Literacy Trust, an independent, UK-based charity that changes lives through literacy. In 2010, he was voted Author of the Year at the Children's Choice Book Awards in New York.

Witch & Wizard

James Patterson

with Gabrielle Charbonnet

A

Published by Young Arrow in 2010

5 7 9 10 8 6

First published in Great Britain in 2009 by
Young Arrow
Random House, 20 Vauxhall Bridge Road,
London SW1V 2SA

www.randomhouse.co.uk

Addresses for companies within The Random House Group Limited can be found at:
www.randomhouse.co.uk/offices.htm

The Random House Group Limited Reg. No. 954009

A CIP catalogue record for this book
is available from the British Library

ISBN 9780099543749

The Random House Group Limited supports The Forest Stewardship
Council (FSC®), the leading international forest certification organisation.
Our books carrying the FSC label are printed on FSC® certified paper.
FSC is the only forest certification scheme endorsed by the leading
environmental organisations, including Greenpeace.
Our paper procurement policy can be found at:
www.randomhouse.co.uk/environment

Printed and bound in Great Britain by Clays Ltd, St Ives Plc

For Andrea Spooner, our hero ☺
—J.P.

Oh, yes—what he said
—G.C.

I believe in aristocracy. . . . Not an aristocracy of power, based upon rank and influence, but an aristocracy of the sensitive, the considerate and the plucky. Its members are to be found in all nations and classes, and all through the ages, and there is a secret understanding between them when they meet. They represent the true human tradition, the one permanent victory of our queer race over cruelty and chaos.

—E. M. Forster, from *Two Cheers for Democracy*

PROLOGUE

YOU'RE NOT IN KANSAS ANYMORE

Wisty

IT'S OVERWHELMING. A city's worth of angry faces staring at me like I'm a wicked criminal—which, I promise you, *I'm not.* The stadium is filled to capacity—past capacity. People are standing in the aisles, the stairwells, on the concrete ramparts, and a few extra thousand are camped out on the playing field. There are no football teams here today. They wouldn't be able to get out of the locker-room tunnels if they tried.

This total abomination is being broadcast on TV and the Internet too. All the useless magazines are here, and the useless newspapers. Yep, I see cameramen in elevated roosts at intervals around the stadium.

There's even one of those remote-controlled cameras that runs around on wires above the field. There it is—hovering just in front of the stage, bobbing slightly in the breeze.

So there are undoubtedly millions more eyes watching

than I can see. But it's the ones here in the stadium that are breaking my heart. To be confronted with tens, maybe even hundreds of thousands, of curious, uncaring, or at least indifferent, faces...talk about *frightening*.

And there are no moist eyes, never mind tears.

No words of protest.

No stomping feet.

No fists raised in solidarity.

No inkling that anybody's even thinking of surging forward, breaking through the security cordon, and carrying my family to safety.

Clearly, this is not a good day for us Allgoods.

In fact, as the countdown ticker flashes on the giant video screens at either end of the stadium, it's looking like this will be our *last* day.

It's a point driven home by the very tall, bald man up in the tower they've erected midfield—he looks like a cross between a Supreme Court chief justice and Ming the Merciless. I know who he is. I've actually met him. He's The One Who Is The One.

Directly behind his Oneness is a huge N.O. banner— THE NEW ORDER.

And then the crowd begins to chant, almost sing, "The One Who Is The One! The One Who Is The One!"

Imperiously, The One raises his hand, and his hooded lackeys on the stage push us forward, at least as far as the ropes around our necks will allow.

I see my brother, Whit, handsome and brave, looking

down at the platform mechanism. Calculating if there's any way to jam it, some means of keeping it from unlatching and dropping us to our neck-snapping deaths. Wondering if there's a last-minute way out of this.

I see my mother crying quietly. Not for herself, of course, but for Whit and me.

I see my father, his tall frame stooped with resignation, smiling at me and my brother — trying to keep our spirits up, reminding us that there's no point in being miserable in our last moments on this planet.

But I'm getting ahead of myself. I'm supposed to be providing an *introduction* here, not the details of our public *execution*.

So let's go back a bit....

BOOK ONE

NO CRIME, JUST PUNISHMENT

BY ORDER OF THE NEW ORDER,

and the Great Wind — The One Who Is

THE ONE —

let it be known that as of

NOW, THIS MOMENT, or

TWELVE O'CLOCK MIDNIGHT,

whichever shall arrive first, following the

SWIFT TRIUMPH of the **ORDER** of the

ONES WHO PROTECT, who have obliterated the

BLIND AND DUMB FORCES of passivity and

complacency **PLAGUING** this world,

ALL CITIZENS *must*, *shall*, and *will* abide by

THESE THREE ORDERS FOR ORDER:

1. All behaviors NOT in keeping with N.O. law, logic, order, and science (including but not limited to theology, philosophy, and IN PARTIC-ULAR the creative and dark arts, et cetera) are hereby ABOLISHED.
2. ALL persons under eighteen years of age will be evaluated for ORDER-LINESS and MUST COMPLY with the prescribed corrective actions.
3. The One Who Is THE ONE grants, appoints, decides, seizes, and exe-cutes at will. All NOT complying shall be SEIZED and/or EXECUTED.

—As declared to The One Who Writes Decrees
by THE ONE WHO IS THE ONE

Chapter 1

Whit

SOMETIMES YOU WAKE UP and the world is just plain different.

The noise of a circling helicopter is what made me open my eyes. A cold, blue-white light forced its way through the blinds and flooded the living room. Almost like it was day.

But it wasn't.

I peered at the clock on the DVD player through blurry eyes: 2:10 a.m.

I became aware of a steady *drub, drub, drub*—like the sound of a heavy heartbeat. Throbbing. Pressing in. Getting closer.

What's going on?

I staggered to the window, forcing my body back to life after two hours of being passed out on the sofa, and peeked through the slats.

And then I stepped back and rubbed my eyes. Hard.

Because there's no way I had seen what I'd seen. And there was no way I had heard what I'd heard.

Was it really the steady, relentless footfall of hundreds of soldiers? Marching on my street in perfect unison?

The road wasn't close enough to the center of town to be on any holiday parade routes, much less to have armed men in combat fatigues coursing down it in the dead of night.

I shook my head and bounced up and down a few times, kind of like I do in my warm-ups. *Wake up, Whit.* I slapped myself for good measure. And then I looked again.

There they were. Soldiers marching down our street. Hundreds of them as clear as day, made visible by a half-dozen truck-mounted spotlights.

Just one thought was running laps inside my head: *This can't be happening. This can't be happening. This can't be happening.*

Then I remembered the elections, the new government, the ravings of my parents about the trouble the country was in, the special broadcasts on TV, the political petitions my classmates were circulating online, the heated debates between teachers at school. None of it meant anything to me until that second.

And before I could piece it all together, the vanguard of the formation stopped in front of my house.

Almost faster than I could comprehend, two armed squads detached themselves from the phalanx and sprinted across the lawn like commandos, one running around the back of the house, the other taking position in front.

I jumped away from the window. I could tell they weren't here to protect me and my family. I had to warn Mom, Dad, Wisty—

But just as I started to yell, the front door was knocked off its hinges.

Chapter 2

Wisty

IT'S QUITE HIDEOUS to get kidnapped in the dead of night, right inside your own home. It went something like this.

I woke to the chaotic crashing of overturning furniture, quickly followed by the sounds of shattering glass, possibly some of Mom's china.

Oh God, Whit, I thought, shaking my head sleepily. My older brother had grown four inches and gained thirty pounds of muscle in the past year. Which made him the biggest and fastest quarterback around, and, I must say, the most intimidating player on our regional high school's undefeated football team.

Off the playing field, though, Whit could be about as clumsy as your average bear—if your average bear were hopped-up on a case of Red Bull and full of himself because he could bench-press 275 and every girl in school thought he was the hunk of all hunks.

I rolled over and pulled my pillow around my head.

14

Even before the drinking started, Whit couldn't walk through our house without knocking something over. Total bull-in-a-china-shop syndrome.

But that wasn't the real problem tonight, I knew.

Because three months ago, his girlfriend, Celia, had literally *vanished* without a trace. And by now everyone was thinking she probably would never come back. Her parents were totally messed up about it, and so was Whit. To be honest, so was I. Celia was—*is*—very pretty, smart, not conceited at all. She's this totally cool girl, even though she has money. Celia's father owns the luxury-car dealership in town, and her mom is a former beauty queen. I couldn't believe something like that would happen to someone like Celia.

I heard my parents' bedroom door open and snuggled back down into my cozy, flannel-sheeted bed.

Next came Dad's booming voice, and he was as angry as I've ever heard him.

"This can't be happening! You have no right to be here. Leave our house *now!*"

I bolted upright, wide awake. Then came more crashing sounds, and I thought I heard someone moan in pain. Had Whit fallen and cracked his head? Had my dad been hurt?

Jeez, Louise, I thought, scrambling out of bed. "I'm coming, Dad! Are you all right? Dad?"

And then the nightmare to start a lifetime of nightmares truly began.

I gasped as my bedroom door crashed open. Two hulking men in dark-gray uniforms burst into my room, glaring at me as if I were a fugitive terrorist-cell operative.

"It's her! Wisteria Allgood!" one said, and a light bright enough to illuminate an airplane hangar obliterated the darkness.

I tried to shield my eyes as my heart kicked into overdrive. "Who are *you?!*" I asked. "What are you doing in *my freaking bedroom?*"

Chapter 3

Wisty

"BE EXTREMELY CAREFUL with her!" one of the humongous men cautioned. They looked like Special Forces operatives with giant white numbers on their uniforms. "You know she can—"

The other nodded, glancing around my room nervously. "You!" he snapped harshly. "Come with us! We're from the New Order. Move one step out of line, and we will punish you severely!"

I stared at him, my head spinning. *The New Order?* These weren't ordinary policemen or EMS personnel.

"Um—I—I—," I stammered. "I need to put on some clothes. Can I...can I have a little privacy?"

"Shut up!" the first commando guy barked. "Grab her! And protect yourself. She's dangerous—all of them are."

"No! Stop! Don't you dare!" I screamed. "Dad! Mom! Whit!"

Then it hit me like a runaway tractor trailer on ice. This was what had happened to Celia, wasn't it?

Oh God! Cold sweat beaded on the back of my neck. *I need to get out of here,* I thought desperately. *Somehow, some way.*

I need to disappear.

Chapter 4

Wisty

THE SERIOUSLY MUSCLE-BOUND MEN in gray suddenly froze, their blocklike heads whipping back and forth like puppets on strings.

"Where is she? She's gone! Vanished! Where'd she go?" one said, his voice hoarse and panicky.

They shone flashlights around the room. One of them dropped to his knees and searched under my bed; the other rushed over to look in my closet.

Where'd *I* go? Were these guys totally *insane*? I was right there. What was going on?

Maybe they were trying to trick me into running for it so they had an excuse to use force. Or maybe they were escapees from an asylum who had come to get me the way they'd come to get poor Celia—

"Wisty!" My mom's anxious shout from the hallway

pierced the fog that had invaded my brain. "Run away, sweetheart!"

"Mom!" I shrieked. The two guys blinked and stepped back in surprise.

"There she is! Grab her! She's right there! Quick, before she disappears again!"

Big klutzy hands grabbed my arms and legs, then my head. "Let me *go!*" I screamed, kicking and struggling. *"Let. Me. Go."*

But their grip was like steel as they dragged me down the hall to the family room and dumped me on the floor like a sack of trash.

I quickly scrambled to my feet, more floodlights whiting out my vision. Then I heard Whit shouting as he was thrown onto the living room floor next to me.

"Whit, what's going on? Who are these . . . *monsters?*"

"Wisty!" he gasped, coherently enough. "You okay?"

"No." I almost cried, but I couldn't, wouldn't, absolutely *refused*, to let them see me wuss out. Every awful true-crime movie I'd ever seen flashed through my head, and my stomach heaved. I nestled close to my brother, who took my hand in his and squeezed.

Suddenly the floodlights turned off, leaving us blinking and shaking.

"Mom?" Whit shouted. *"Dad?"* If my brother hadn't been stone-cold sober already, he sure was now.

I gasped. My parents were standing there, still in their

rumpled pajamas, but held from behind like they were dangerous criminals. Sure, we lived on the wrong side of the tracks, but no one in our family had ever been in trouble before.

Not that I knew of anyway.

Chapter 5

Wisty

ONE OF THE MOST TERRIFYING THINGS in the world you can never hope to see is your parents, wide-eyed, helpless, and truly scared out of their wits.

My parents. I thought they could protect us from anything. They were different from other parents…so smart, gentle, accepting, knowing…and I could tell at this moment that they knew something Whit and I didn't.

They know what is going on. And they're terrified of it, whatever it is.

"Mom…?" I asked, staring hard into her eyes, trying to get any message I could, any signal about what I should do now.

As I looked at Mom, I had a flash, a collage of memories. She and Dad saying stuff like "You and Whit are special, honey. *Really* special. Sometimes people are afraid of those who are different. Being afraid makes them angry and unreasonable." But all parents thought their kids were special, right? "I mean, you're *really* special, Wisty," Mom had said once, taking my chin in her palm. "Pay attention, dear."

Then three more figures stepped forward from the shadows. Two of them had guns on their belts. This was really getting out of hand. Guns? Soldiers? In our house? In a free country? In the middle of the night? A *school* night, even.

"Wisteria Allgood?" As they moved into the light, I saw two men and...

Byron Swain?

Byron was a kid from my high school, a year older than I, a year younger than Whit. As far as I knew, we both hated his guts. *Everyone* did.

"What are *you* doing here, Swain?" Whit snarled. "Get out of our house."

Byron. It was like his parents knew he'd turn out to be a snot, so they'd named him appropriately.

"Make me," Byron said to Whit, then he gave a smarmy, oily smile, vividly bringing to life all the times I'd seen him in school and thought, *What a total butt.* He had slicked-back brown hair, perfectly combed, and cold hazel eyes. Like an iguana's.

So this jerk extraordinaire was flanked by two commandos in dark uniforms, shiny black boots that came above their knees, and metal helmets. The entire world was turning upside down, with me in my ridiculous pink kitty jammies.

"What are you *doing* here?" I echoed Whit.

"Wisteria Allgood," Byron monotoned like a bailiff, and pulled out an actual scroll of official-looking paper. "The New Order is taking you into custody until your trial. You are hereby accused of being a witch."

My jaw dropped. "*A witch?* Are you *nuts?*" I shrieked.

Chapter 6

Wisty

THE TWO GOONS IN GRAY marched toward me. Instinctively I held up both my hands. Amazingly the New Order soldiers stopped in their tracks, and I felt a surge of strength—if only for a moment.

"Did we just go back in *time?*" I squealed. "Last I looked this was the twenty-first century, not the *seventeenth!*"

I narrowed my eyes. Another glance at that smarmy Byron Swain in his shiny boots spurred me on further. "You can't just come in here, grabbing us—"

"Whitford Allgood," Byron Swain rudely interrupted, continuing to read in an official tone from his scroll, "you are hereby accused of being a wizard. You will be held in custody until your trial."

He smirked tauntingly at Whit, even though under normal circumstances my brother could have picked him up and wrung his neck like a chicken's. I guess confidence isn't hard to come by when you have armed soldiers at your beck and call.

"Wisty is right. This is utterly crazy!" my brother snapped. His face was flushed, his blue eyes shining with anger. "There's no such thing as witches or wizards! Fairy tales are a load of crap. Who do you think you are, you creepy little weasel? A character from *Gary Blotter and the Guild of Rejects*?"

My parents looked horrified—but not actually *surprised*. So WTH?

I remembered slightly odd lessons my folks had given us throughout our childhood: about plants and herbs, and the weather—always the weather—and how to concentrate, how to focus. They also taught us a lot about artists we'd never study at school too, like Wiccan Trollack, De Glooming, and Frieda Halo. As I got older, I guess I thought my parents were maybe just being a little hippie-dippy or something. But I never really questioned this stuff. Was it all somehow related to tonight?

Byron looked at Whit calmly. "According to the New Order Code, you may each take one possession from the house. I don't approve, but that's the letter of the law, and I will abide by it, of course."

Under the watchful eye of the gray-garbed soldiers, Mom quickly moved to the bookshelf. She hesitated a moment, glancing at Dad.

He nodded, and then she grabbed an old drumstick that had sat on the shelf for as long as I could remember. Family legend has it that my wild-man grandfather, back in the day, actually leaped onstage at a Groaning Bones concert and took it from the drummer. Mom held it out to me.

"Please," she said with a sniffle, "just take it, Wisteria. *Take* the drumstick. I love you so much, sweetheart."

Then my father reached for an unlabeled book I'd never seen before—a journal or something—on the shelf next to his reading chair. He thrust it into Whit's hands. "I love you, Whit," he said.

A drumstick and an old book? How about a drum to go with that stick? Couldn't they give us a family heirloom or something vaguely personal to cheer us up? Or maybe Whit's mammoth stash of nonperishable junk food for a handy-dandy sugar rush?

Not one part of this waking nightmare made any sense.

Byron snatched the tattered old book from Whit and flipped through it.

"It's blank," he said, surprised.

"Yeah, like your social calendar," said Whit. The guy can be funny, I admit, but his timing sometimes leaves something to be desired.

Byron slammed the book against Whit's face, snapping his head sideways as if it were on a swivel.

Whit's eyes bulged and he sprang toward Byron, only to have the soldiers body-block him.

Byron stood behind the bigger men, smiling wickedly. "Take them to the van," Byron said, and the soldiers grabbed me again.

"No! Mom! Dad! Help!" I shrieked and tried to pull away, but it was like wriggling in a steel trap. Rock-hard arms dragged me toward the door. I managed to twist my neck around for one last look back at my parents, searing my memory with the horror on their faces, the tears in their eyes.

And right then I felt this whooshing sensation, as if a stiff, hot wind were blowing up against me. In an instant, blood rushed to my head, my cheeks flooded with heat, and sweat seemed to leap from my skin and sizzle. There was a buzzing all around me, and then...

You won't believe me, but it's true. I swear.

I saw—and felt—foot-long *flames* burst out of every pore in my body.

Chapter 7

Wisty

I HEARD SCARED-SILLY SCREAMS everywhere, even from the commandos, as I stood gaping at the orange-yellow tongues of flame shooting off me.

If you think that's weird, listen to this: after that first moment, I didn't feel the least bit hot. And when I looked at my hands, they were still skin-colored, not red or blackened.

It was...far-out, actually.

Suddenly one of the soldiers swung Mom's porcelain vase at me. I was drenched—and the flames were gone.

Byron Swain's cronies were stamping out the drapes and some smoldering spots on the carpet where the soldiers had dropped me.

But then Byron himself—who'd apparently fled the house during my immolation—reappeared in the doorway, his face faintly green. He pointed a spindly, shaking finger at me. "See?! See?! *See?!*" he shouted hoarsely. "Lock her up! Shoot her if you have to. Whatever it takes!"

I was suddenly overcome by this horrible, stomach-twisting feeling that this night had been inevitable — that it was always meant to be part of my life story.

But I had no idea why I thought that, or what it meant exactly.

Chapter 8

Whit

I HADN'T HALLUCINATED before, but when I saw Wisty burst into flame, that's what I suspected it was—a stress-induced hallucination.

I mean, I expect even well-rested, grounded, grief-free people wouldn't just go, *Oh, look at that, my little sister just turned herself into a human torch.* Am I right?

But pretty soon—what with the heat and the smoke and our living room drapes catching on fire—it started to dawn on me that this was really happening.

Then I thought the New Order thugs had *set* her on fire. So I guess that's how I manage to muster enough rage to break free of their grasp. And I swear I would've decked the creeps if I hadn't had to scramble madly to help put her out first.

Then utter chaos broke loose in our house.

I've never been in a tornado before, but that's immediately what I thought was happening. The windows suddenly exploded, and the wind poured in with the force of an angry mountain river, hurling things—broken glass, floor lamps, side tables—around the living room.

I couldn't hear anything over the noise, and it was raining so hard that the water itself—to say nothing of the debris it was carrying—stung like a cloud of bees getting shot through a leaf blower.

And of course I couldn't see anything either. To open your eyes would have been asking to be permanently blinded by wood splinters, glass shards, and plaster chunks.

So my breaking free from the thugs didn't do me a bit of good. We were all clinging to the floor, to the walls, to anything that seemed more solid than ourselves, just trying not to get sucked out a window and flung to our deaths.

I tried yelling for Wisty, but I couldn't even hear my own voice.

And then—in an instant—everything was still and quiet.

I moved my face out of the crook of my arm . . . and took in a sight I won't forget for the rest of my life.

A tall, bald, extremely imposing man was standing there in the middle of our demolished living room. Not scary, you think? Think again.

This is the dude who turns out to be evil personified.

"Hello, Allgood family," he said in a quiet, forceful tone that made me pay very close attention to every word. "I am The One Who Is The One. Perhaps you've heard of me?"

My father spoke up. "We know who you are. We're

not afraid of you, though, and we won't bend to your ugly rules."

"I wouldn't expect you to bend to any rules, Benjamin. Or you, Eliza," he said to my mother. "Aspiring deviants like you always value freedom above all else. But it doesn't matter whether you accept this new reality or not. It's the youngins I'm here to see. This is a command performance, you understand. I *command*, they obey."

Now the bald dude looked at my little sister and me, and he smiled quite congenially, even warmly.

"I will make this simple for the two of you. All you have to do is renounce your former existence—your freedoms, your way of life, and your parents in particular—and you will be spared. You will not be harmed if you obey the rules. Not a hair on your heads will be touched. I promise. Renounce your former ways and your parents. That's all. Simple as apple pie."

"No way!" I yelled at the guy.

"Not going to happen. Ever," Wisty said. "We renounce *you*, Your Baldness, Your Terribleness!"

He actually chuckled at that, which totally caught me off guard.

"Whitford Allgood," The One said, and looked deeply into my eyes. Something strange happened then—I couldn't move or speak, only listen. It was the scariest thing yet that night.

"You're a beautiful boy, I must say, Whitford. Tall and blond, slender yet well-muscled, perfectly proportioned.

You have your mother's eyes. I know that you were a very good boy until recently, ever since the sad and *unfortunate* disappearance of your girlfriend and soul mate, Celia."

Frustrated rage boiled up inside me. What did he know about Celia? He'd smirked when he spoke of her disappearance. He knew something. He was taunting me.

"The question is," he went on, "*can* you be good again? Can you learn to obey the rules?"

He threw up his hands. "Don't know?!" he exclaimed even as my paralyzed mouth prevented me from screaming the string of choice obscenities I was trying to fling at him. Then he turned to Wisty. "Wisteria Allgood, I know all about you too. Disobedient, recalcitrant, a truant, over two weeks of detention due to be served at your high school. The question is, can you *ever* be good? Can you possibly learn to obey?"

He stared at Wisty, silent, waiting.

And in true Wisty fashion, she did the most adorable little curtsy, then proclaimed, "Of course, sir, your every waking wish is my command."

Wisty stopped her sarcastic speech rather suddenly, and I realized that he'd paralyzed her too. Then The One Who Is The One turned to his guards. "Take them away! They shall never see their parents again. Nor shall you, Ben and Eliza, see your very special offspring until the day you all die."

Chapter 9

Whit

WISTY AND I WERE in a big black van that had no windows. My heart was thumping like an epileptic rabbit's, and my vision was nearly whited-out with adrenaline. It took every shred of sanity I had left not to throw myself at the van walls. I pictured myself smashing my head against the metal, kicking open the back doors, helping Wisty out, and escaping into the night...

Only none of that happened.

As far as I knew, I was *not* a wizard, and not a super-hero either. I was just a high school kid who'd been ripped out of his home.

I looked over at poor Wisty, but I was barely able to make out her profile in the dark. Her wet hair dripped onto my arm, and I realized she was shivering badly. Maybe with cold, maybe with shock, maybe with cold and shock and total freaking disbelief.

I put my arms around her bony shoulders, awkwardly because I was now handcuffed. I had to slip her head between my arms. I couldn't remember the last time I'd done that, except maybe to pin her down because she'd gotten into my stuff, or when I'd caught her spying on me and . . . Celia.

I couldn't think about her right now or I might completely lose it.

"You okay?" I said. Wisty appeared to be totally uncharred—no roasting-hot-dog smell or anything.

"Of course I'm not okay," she said, leaving the usual "you idiot" off the end of her sentence. "They must have dumped something flammable on me. I'm not burned, though."

"I didn't see them spray anything on you," I said. "It was like, boom—flamesicle!" I mustered a weak smile. "'Course, I always knew your hair was dangerous." Wisty is a real carrottop—with thick, wavy bright-red hair that she hates but that I think is kind of cool.

Wisty was too freaked to take the bait about her hair—at first. "Whit, what's going on? What does schmucky-*beyond*-schmucky Byron Swain have to do with it? What's happening to us? And to Mom and Dad?"

"It's got to be some kind of terrible mistake. Mom and Dad never hurt a fly." I remembered my parents then, held fast and helpless, and I had to swallow my rage.

Just then, the van came to a lurching halt. I tensed, staring hard at the doors, primed to barrel somebody down. Even in handcuffs. Even if it was a giant, steroid-enhanced soldier.

I wasn't going to let them hurt my sister. I wasn't going to be a goody-goody and obey their stupid rules.

Chapter 10

Whit

IT WAS LIKE WE'D WOKEN UP, and suddenly we were living in a totalitarian state.

The first thing I saw looming over me were dozens of flapping flags and the big black block letters N.O.

NO. It seemed totally appropriate, even a touch poetic. *NO.*

Wisty and I were outside a huge, windowless building, surrounded by a chain-link, concertina-wire-topped fence. Giant letters that read NEW ORDER REFORMATORY were engraved in a stone rising high above the steel entryway.

Then the doors creaked open, and I realized that barreling our way to safety probably wasn't going to work out so great. *Ten* more guards—these in black uniforms—came out the front, joined the two drivers, and formed a semicircle around the rear of the van.

"Okay, now watch 'em closely," I heard one say. "You know, they're—"

"Yeah, we know," said another cranky voice, one of the drivers. "I got the burns to prove it."

I didn't even bother struggling as those brainless storm troopers hauled us forward, then dragged us through the tall barbed-wire gate.

I'm pretty big—six feet one, 190 pounds—but these guys acted like I was a sack of popcorn. Wisty and I tried to stay on our feet, but they kept yanking us off balance.

"We can walk!" Wisty yelled. "We're still conscious!"

"We can change all that," said one of the thug guards.

I tried, "Listen, listen, you've got the wrong—"

The guard next to me raised his billy club, and I shut up midsquawk. They pushed us up the concrete steps, through the heavy steel doors, and into a brightly lit foyer. It looked like a prison, with a burly guard behind a thick glass window, a locked gate, and another guard with a billy club at the ready.

I heard a loud buzz, and the gate opened.

"Don't you guys feel kind of dumb?" I said. "I mean, a dozen giant men, just for us two kids—it's kind of embarrassing. Wouldn't you—*ow!*" A guard had jabbed my ribs, hard, with his wooden baton.

"Start thinking about your upcoming interrogation," the guard said. "Talk, or die. Your choice, kiddies."

Chapter 11

Wisty

IT WAS BEGINNING TO FEEL like this sickening nightmare was for real, and now I wasn't even going to be allowed the small comfort of going through it in my old pink PJs. They made us change into gray-striped prison jumpsuits that looked like something out of World War II. Whit's jumpsuit fit him — guess he was standard-prisoner size — but mine hung on me like a sail on a windless day.

My funky PJs had been my last connection to home. Without them, the only thing I had from my former life was the drumstick.

The drumstick. *Why a drumstick, Mom?* I missed her already and felt a deep anxiety creep in when I wondered what they'd done with her and Dad.

"Don't pull her arm like that!" Whit snapped at my guard. He was right. It felt like my arm was about to pop out of its socket.

"Shut up, wizard," growled the surly guard, dragging

us through yet another electronic gate marked PROPERTY OF THE NEW ORDER. Then we were in an enormous hall, five stories high, surrounded on all sides by cages and barred cells.

For criminals.

And us. Me and my brother. Can you imagine? No—you probably can't. How could anybody in their right mind imagine this?

One of the cell doors slid open, and the guards threw me inside. I fell, hitting my knees and hands hard on the cement floor.

"*Wisty!*" Whit shouted as they hauled him past my door, which immediately slid shut. I pressed my face against the bars, trying to see where they were taking Whit. They shoved him in the cell next to mine.

"Wisty, you okay?" Whit called over right away.

"Sort of," I said, examining my scraped knees. "If I'm allowed to totally change what 'okay' means."

"We'll get out of here," he said. I could hear the braveness and anger in his voice. "This is all just a stupid mistake."

"Au contraire, my naive amigo," said a voice from the cell on the other side of Whit.

"*What? Who are you?*" Whit asked.

I strained to hear his words.

"I'm prisoner number 450209A," said the voice. "Trust me, there's been no mistake. And they didn't forget to read you your rights. And they aren't going to give you a lawyer or a phone call. And your mama and papa aren't coming to get you. *Ever.* And that's a long, long time."

"What do you know about it?" I shouted.

"Look, how old are you?" said the voice.

"I'm almost eighteen," Whit said, "and my sister's fifteen."

"Well, I'm thirteen," he offered, "so you'll fit right in here."

And then I looked across at all the cells on the other side of the block. I saw face after face, one scared kid after another. All wearing too-big prison jumpsuits.

It looked like this whole jail was full of *kids,* nothing but kids.

Chapter 12

Wisty

"YUP, IT'S PRETTY much just us kids around here these days," said the voice from the far cell. "I've been here nine days—I was one of the first. But in the last three days, this rat hole has really filled up."

"Do you have any idea what's going on?" Whit asked softly, so as not to attract a guard's attention.

"Not a whole lot, jefe. But I heard some of the guards talking about a clean sweep," the voice said quietly, close to the bars. "You remember hearing about the New Order?"

"Yeah," I joined in, "but I wasn't really paying attention."

"Okay, so you've been living inside your head...somewhere dark and nasty," said the voice. "But, if it's any consolation, so was most of the rest of the country. See, the New Order is the political party that's been winning all the elections. They're in charge now. In just a few months they've gutted the old government and instituted the Council of Ones. Heard of them? The One In Command, The

One Who Judges, The One Who Imprisons, The One Who Assigns Numbers, The One Who Is The One, blah, blah."

"Okay, so, the New Order. Politics," said Whit. "What's that got to do with us?"

"They're the Law *and* they're the Order, amigos. They're The Ones who put us here, and they're The Ones who decide what to do with us."

"But why are they doing these unspeakable things to *kids?*" I spoke up again.

"Because we talk back? Because we're hard to control? Because we have an *imagination?* Because we're not brainwashed yet? Who knows? Why don't you ask The One Who Judges . . . *at your trial!*"

I squished myself against the bars as hard as I could, trying to see through to Whit. "*Trial?* What trial?" I asked. "We're going to trial? For what?"

Wham!

A guard had sneaked up, grabbed my arm through the bars, and twisted it the wrong way. "If you keep talking to the other prisoners, I'll put you all in solitary!" he growled.

He gave my arm another hard, agonizing twist and laughed like some crazy old cartoon villain. I was so mad I wanted to tear the bars down and kick him in the throat—and all of a sudden an electric rush traveled up my body.

Uh-oh.

The next thing I knew, I was watching the guard

through a sheet of flames. Flames that were coming from...me. *Again*.

"Agh!" the guard shouted as the sleeve and pants leg of his uniform caught fire. He ran and grabbed an extinguisher, spraying himself as a team of his buddies converged on my cell.

"Wisty!" Whit yelled. "Duck!"

I threw my hands up to cover my face as I was drenched with flame-smothering foam. Correction: *Wisty-smothering* foam. Then suddenly the flames were out and I looked like a flocked Christmas tree, a lemon-meringue pie, a red-haired zombie snowman, risen from the dead.

"No more tricks," said the guard hoarsely. "You're coming with me."

Four New Order guards with bats and stun guns stomped in and grabbed my arms, hauling me out to the walkway. Four more creeps were opening Whit's cell.

By the time the guards shoved us into a room marked INTERROGATION, I was ready to show The One Who Interrogates just why I had two weeks of detention racked up at my school.

But when the door opened, it was just that spud, Byron Swain, followed by a pair of guards. "Miss me?" he asked with a sickening grin.

Chapter 13

Whit

BYRON'S INSURANCE-SALESMAN HAIRCUT, colorful polo shirts, and ironed chinos—but most of all his know-it-all attitude—had marked him as a major kiss-up back at school. This close, his face looked pinched and mean, like that of a pet ferret with hall-monitor aspirations.

Tossing a folder on the metal table, he nodded to the two guards, and they stepped back against the wall.

"Have you been working out, Swain?" I asked, clenching my fists. "I mean, it doesn't look it, but don't you need to have at least *six* guards backing you up?"

Swain's face flushed bright red. "We both know why you're here," he said, pacing. "Hmmm?"

The little twerp was trying to sound authoritative and manly, but his naturally whiny, nasal voice cracked through at the end of every sentence. His cold eyes didn't leave my face. "The sooner you admit your secrets and tell us what we want to know, the better it will be for you and your freaky fire-breathing sister."

"Got no idea what you're talking about, skippy," I said.

His weaselly eyes narrowed. Suddenly he leaned on the table, getting nose-to-nose with me.

"You can back off the drama-queen performance, okay?" I told him.

"Are you two miscreants protecting someone?!" he snapped, ignoring my taunts. "Well, *they're* certainly not protecting you. Your good friends have already told us everything we need to know. We're aware of your drinking problems, *Whitford*. And we hardly need corroboration of your sister's pyromaniac tendencies. But those are just the license plates on the truckload of information your 'friends' delivered up. It was beautiful. I mean, a handful of marbles couldn't have rolled any easier."

"That right?" I said. "Like, they told you where I keep my stash of doughnut holes? My gaming cheat codes? The D on my last bio test that my folks don't know about? Somehow, getting grounded isn't the threat it used to be!"

"You almost flunked biology?" Wisty whispered as I watched a vein appear in Byron's forehead. "Cool."

"Shut up, freak!" he roared at Wisty, who just stuck out her tongue. "I saw what you did earlier! You burst into flames! And you weren't even hurt afterward! If that's not sick and wrong, I don't know what is! You think it's bad, being here in this wussy prison? It will get a lot worse! Trust me on that, you deviants—a *lot* worse."

"You know, Byron," Wisty said in her most insulting la-di-da voice, "*you're* the freak, actually. We could put *you* on our secret voodoo witchcrafty to-do list."

At that, Swain snapped. Lunging across the table, he grabbed Wisty's arm so hard she yelped. And then, the weirdest thing—and that's saying something—a flash of blinding light leaped between my sister's free hand and Byron's chest.

The creep squealed like a guinea pig and was thrown backward, falling on his butt near the astounded guards.

My eyes nearly falling out of my head in disbelief, I looked over at my sister and realized she had just hit Byron with a lightning bolt.

Lightning. A small bolt, sure, but *lightning!* From her *fingertips!*

"More proof!" Byron squeaked, his voice sounding extracrispy and his face almost purple. He was rubbing his chest, obviously horrified by the burn mark on his shirt. "You *are* a witch! You'll be locked up forever!" He got to his unsteady feet and staggered from the interrogation room.

"You're throwing lightning at people now?" I asked Wisty. "I mean, *whoa.*"

Chapter 14

Whit

I MUST HAVE FALLEN OFF to sleep soon after Spud Swain's visit. Then I woke in my cell with hot tears rolling down my cheeks.

It's not that I'm a total wuss, though I can be during sappy movies sometimes. I was crying because I'd just talked to Celia—in a dream, I guess it was a dream, but it felt so real to me. No, it *was* real. I remembered hugging Celia tight to my chest like we were on the most heart-breaking date of all time.

"Hi, Whit, missed you," she said, like it was perfectly normal for me to be seeing her again after all these months with her missing. "I'm trying to act casual, and failing pretty bad," she said with a gentle smile. "Sorry."

"Celia, are you okay? What happened to you?" I blurted out. My heart was pounding like a bass drum.

"We'll get to all that. I promise. The question is, are *you* okay? Is Wisty?"

49

"Sure—you know me, Celia, I can roll with it. And Wisty is tough as nails. She's *smoking,* actually." I chuckled weakly at my own joke. "I guess we're a little weirded out, though."

Celia smiled again, and I just about couldn't stand it. I'd had no idea how much I'd missed that incredible grin of hers until right now. And she was prettier than ever—if that was even possible. Smooth skin, long dark curls, the brightest blue eyes that always told me the truth, even if I didn't want to hear it.

"You look great, Whit—for somebody who's been kidnapped, beaten up, and jailed illegally." Now a half smile.

"Forget about me. I want to hear everything about you. Celia, *what* is going on? Where did you go?"

She winced, then her head slowly moved from side to side, and tears rolled from her eyes. "That's a tough question. And I know I just got here, Whit, but I really have to go now. I just had to make sure you were okay. And Whit—it's hard to believe *I'm* saying this to *you,* of all people—you really have to hang tough. You and Wisteria. Otherwise you'll both be dead."

Then Celia was gone—I was wide awake—and I'd been warned about what to do next.

Hang tough.

Chapter 15

Wisty

I USED TO THINK detention was kinda fun. A badge of honor, almost. Man, how quickly things can change.

This was the real thing.

My old life, and the days of recklessly skipping class, felt like a million worlds away now. I missed it, and our house, and especially our mom and dad, so badly that I felt like I was going to lose it.

I stared at the ceiling and daydreamed, remembering...

How Mom used to lie in bed with Whit and me when we were really little, and she'd laugh and laugh, and tell us that she was teaching us how to love laughter, because it was one of the very best things in life, maybe the best.

And...

How Dad always said he had to be our father, not our friend—and that there was an important distinction between the two—but somehow he ended up being our best friend anyway.

And...

How we went on all of those great family trips to art museums such as the Betelheim and the Britney. And then those potentially corny family camping trips, one every season—no matter how cold or rainy it was—and we learned how to survive in the world, but more than that, to love what was out there, just waiting to be discovered.

Like this great oak tree that was in our yard—the one that Whit and I learned to climb almost as soon as we could walk... and *fall*.

And then... there were two guards at my door.

With handcuffs.

And leg shackles.

"For me?" I beamed at the two creeps. "Aw, you shouldn't have."

Amazingly, neither of them thought that was the least bit funny.

"Come on, witch!" one guard snapped. "It's your day in court. Now you get to meet The One Who Judges... and you're definitely not going to like him."

"Of course," said the other guard, "that's only fair—he's definitely not going to like you either."

The guards thought *that* was hysterical.

Chapter 16

Whit

SUNLIGHT—the first we'd seen in what seemed like ages—came streaming through thirty-feet-high windows in the courtroom, almost blinding us. I squinted and tried to shield my eyes, only to whack my forehead with my handcuffs. *Klutz much?*

I had thought by now I'd be hard to shock, but I couldn't believe the scene in front of me.

A mammoth portrait of The One Who Is The One hung at the center of the room, like he was a conquering general or the emperor. There was a huge metal cage in front of the judge's desk—yes, a cage, like for shark diving. One guard held the door open, and the other one pushed us into it.

Into a *cage.*

In a courtroom.

"I'm almost getting used to looking through bars," Wisty said, sounding resigned. Not like Wisty at all.

"Don't say that," I whispered sharply. "We're getting out of this madhouse. I promise."

But how? I scanned the courtroom. Surrounding us was an impenetrable wall of indifference, even hatred. Plus at least a dozen armed guards.

A judge — The One Who Judges, I assumed — glowered from a high platform right in front of us, his thin, greasy gray hair stuck down to his scalp.

On the right-hand side of the courtroom, behind a low wall, a jury stared vacantly at us. They were all grown-ups, all men, and apparently they seemed to think two innocent kids appearing on trial in a cage was nothing unusual.

So it was official now: the world had gone totally crazy.

Chapter 17

Whit

THE ONE WHO JUDGES put tiny glasses on his long, beaked nose and scowled down at us. I read his gold plaque: JUDGE EZEKIEL UNGER.

He picked up a piece of paper. "Whitford Allgood!" he read in a stinging voice. "Wisteria Allgood! This trial is convened because you are accused of the most serious crimes against the New Order!" He glared at us.

There was a standing-room-only audience of grown-ups behind us. I turned to see the crowd better. The few of them who looked at me were cold-eyed and full of hatred.

I rubbed my forehead against my arm as the judge angrily read a bunch of legal-sounding gibberish.

I peered at the jury—surely some of them had to feel sorry for two kids who looked hungry and dirty? Kids in handcuffs, in a cage, with no lawyer? But their faces were frozen in expressions of condemnation. It was as if they were being paid to dislike us. Was there some neon sign above our heads that read SCOWL instead of APPLAUSE, like on the live TV shows?

"What have we done?" Wisty suddenly yelled at the judge. "Just tell us that. What are we accused of?"

"Silence!" the judge shouted. "Listen, you contemptuous girl! You are a most dangerous threat to everything that is proper and right and good. We know this from police witnesses to your recent perpetrations of the dark arts. We know this from innumerable investigations undertaken by the New Order's Investigative Security Agency, and we know this, most fundamentally, because of the Prophecy."

My mouth dropped open as I saw the jury nodding.

"Prophecy?" I scoffed. "I promise you — my sister and I are nowhere in the Good Book. Get real, Ezekiel."

The courtroom gasped. "Blasphemer!" a woman cried out, and shook her fist at us.

The bailiff rushed toward me with his billy club raised, and I lifted my eyebrows in mock fear. *Uh, I'm in a cage, stupid. The bars work both ways.*

Judge Unger continued, "Therefore, based on the preponderance of evidence —"

"Look, whatever the charges, we plead *not guilty!*" I yelled, grabbing the bars of the cage despite my handcuffs and shaking them with all my strength. Which I guess wasn't the smartest thing.

Smack! The bailiff raked his nightstick across my knuckles. Wisty gasped, and I barely managed to swallow a scream of pain.

The One Who Judges literally leaped out of his chair and leaned over his desk, practically within spitting distance. "That's showing those vermin! Well done, bailiff! That's the only way to deal with this kind of filth! If you spare the rod, you spoil the deviants!"

His face was mottled purple and white, his eyes bugging out of his head.

"How say you to these charges?" he yelled at us.

Dumbfounded, Wisty and I replied, *"Not guilty!"*

The judge turned away from us. "Gentlemen of the jury, with that statement, the defendants stand in clear contempt of your will and this court's mission. They mock us. They flout the standards of the glorious New Order! I ask you, *what is your verdict?*"

"That's it?" I yelled from the cage. "That's our trial?"

"You've got to be kidding!" screamed Wisty. "That's not fair."

Smack! went the bailiff's nightstick. *Smack! Smack! Smack!*

Chapter 18

Whit

THIS WHOLE CRAZY THING was happening so fast.

In ordinary, *lawful* trials, one juror stands and reads the verdict from a sheet of paper that often shakes in his or her hand. But this was a travesty of justice. This jury simply held their fists out. We watched as the men, one by one, turned their hands thumbs-down. All of them. Unanimous.

Of course, in ordinary trials, there are also lawyers and due process and principles such as innocent until proven guilty, and things like that. Welcome to the New World Order, I guess.

Judge Unger banged his gavel so hard that Wisty and I jumped. "Guilty as charged!" he roared, and my breath froze in my chest.

"You, Wisteria Allgood, are hereby determined by the New Order to be a witch! You, Whitford Allgood, are determined to be a wizard!"

Wisty and I could only stare up at him in shock and disbelief. But he had saved his best line for last.

"Both of which are punishable by hanging...until *dead*."

Chapter 19

Wisty

HANGING UNTIL DEAD?

This isn't real.

My ears started to buzz.

This can't be real. This doesn't happen. This has to be a nightmare.

My chest tightened up. The room started to go green. And fuzzy.

And then I heard Whit's voice. Like it was coming to me down a long tunnel. Finally, he shook my shoulder.

"Hang in there, Wisty," he said quietly. I blinked and focused on his face. "Love you."

I nodded. Whit didn't think he was special, but his words and his touch were like a magic bullet of strength. I could breathe now. "Love you too," I whispered. "More than I ever knew before."

I inhaled deeply and braced myself for what Judge Unger had to say next.

"Unfortunately, executions are not allowed until said criminal is eighteen years of age."

The buzzing returned to my ears, the fuzziness to my sight.

Whit would be eighteen in less than a month!

I wondered why I wasn't feeling a little *flameish* or *lightningy* right about now. I wanted to lash out at this judge so much that it hurt.

"Therefore, both of you will be held in the state penitentiary"—he continued gravely, and then smiled—"for the time being." He nodded at the bailiff in the courtroom and said, "Take them out of my sight."

The guards removed us from the cage—sort of clumsily, I might add, since Whit was thrashing like a rabid animal. "You're making a terrible mistake!" he yelled. "This is insane! You'll be disbarred! This isn't legal!"

"Shut up, wizard!" the judge screamed, and suddenly hurled his gavel at Whit.

Whit held up his cuffed hands, and then—

The gavel just hung there in midair for a good five seconds—maybe six inches from Whit's face—then dropped heavily to the floor.

The courtroom was completely silent for a moment. Then chaos took over. Angry voices howled, "Witch! Wizard! Put them to death! Execute them both!"

And they really did mean *us*, didn't they? Wisty and Whit. The witch and wizard.

Chapter 20

Wisty

THE ANGRY CHANTING and taunting of the courtroom crowd filled our ears as Whit and I were dragged and shoved down a long, narrow hallway and through throngs of perfect strangers, all thirsty for blood—*our* blood.

Talk about a way to kill your faith in humanity.

A few days ago, it seemed like the worst thing that could happen to me was waking up with a giant zit during school-picture day. How could life as I'd known it change so quickly and bizarrely? My brother and I had just been *sentenced to death.*

The horrid word "execution" kept bouncing around inside my head, sending me into a daze as Whit and I were shoved into another van.

I thought of all the people I'd learned about in school who'd been executed or assassinated. I came up with almost a dozen. But they were all political or religious leaders. And I was just Wisteria Allgood. I wasn't powerful enough to scare people. Was I? I was not a hero, a prophet, a saint, or a leader of any kind. *It made no sense.*

And then, another horrible thing. Stunning. Something that changed my mind about the worst thing that could ever happen to me.

As we rode through the city, we kept our faces pressed against a tiny window in the foul-smelling van—desperate for sunlight, if nothing else—watching the city streets go by, watching soldiers, soldiers everywhere.

Until we saw a new sign being constructed by workmen.

WANTED FOR TREASON
AND CRIMINAL PRACTICE OF FOUL ARTS

Underneath the words were black-and-white photographs of Mom and Dad.

And then the kicker:

DEAD OR ALIVE!

"They got away," Whit whispered. "They're out there somewhere. Somehow, we'll find them."

BOOK TWO

VERY DICKENSIAN

Chapter 21

Wisty

WHEN THE UGLY BLACK NEW ORDER VAN finally stopped, it was raining hard outside and the wind howled. We were parked in front of another large building, this one with high stone walls that looked charred, kind of like an old factory. Stains over the doorway revealed where foot-high letters used to be. They had read GENERAL BOWEN STATE PSYCHIATRIC HOSPITAL.

For a moment, I got the idea this nightmare might actually make sense. *That's it!* I thought with a breath of hope. *I'm psychotic! Everything that's just happened has been a clever collection of my own delusions.*

That would explain the fire . . . the strange and random appearance of Byron Swain . . . the death sentence for being a witch.

The good doctors'll treat me here, Mom and Dad will come get me when I'm well, and everything will be fine again. I'm just psychotic, is all. No biggie.

I smiled involuntarily at the thought. Whit looked over at me like I was—not surprisingly—certifiably insane. I sure hoped so.

"What's with you? You're half smiling. Why? This looks like a hellhouse." He grimaced.

"Well, what were you expecting?" I said with a titter. "Warm and fuzzy?"

We were whisked out of the van and past the stone walls. "Move it!" The guard jabbed me in the back with his baton, pushing me into a wide, dark hallway. One faint fluorescent light flickered at its distant end. A light at the end of the tunnel? I doubted *that*.

"Will I be treated here?" I took the chance of asking. "When can I meet with the doctor?"

Whit twisted his head around and gave me another confused look.

"This is a jail of the New Order, girlie," one of the guards said, sounding both brusque and nervous. "For *dangerous* criminals. Like you two."

We were pushed into a very dim stairwell, lit by only the faintest light seeping under the doorways at each landing. My legs were shivery, probably because we hadn't had anything real to eat since oh-nightmare-thirty. The guards marched us up higher and higher until I surrendered to fatigue and quit counting the landings.

Finally we entered yet another dark hallway with what looked to be an ancient nurses' station front and center. A woman inside was slouched over her desk, engrossed in *New Order Administrator* magazine. She must have been enormously tall, because even though she was sitting, she was able to look down at me.

"Yes?" she croaked like a frog who'd smoked too many cigarettes. "Why are you bothering me?"

Dark eyes, without any whites, bored into mine. She had a crooked nose and a pointy chin with a huge mole that had wiry black hairs growing out of it. Heck, if the New Order was really looking to arrest witches...

"Two more despicable degenerates for you, Matron," announced one of the guards. "A witch and a wizard."

My stomach sank down into my socks. My short-lived fantasy of psychosis was officially over.

You know life really sucks when you're desperately wishing to be institutionalized, drugged, or shocked back to reality. I'd gladly take a lobotomy at this point. I guess that's what you're faced with when freedom isn't even a pipe dream any longer.

Give me lobotomy or give me death!

Chapter 22

Whit

"POLICE MUST BE DREDGING every rancid trash pile in the country," the Matron snarled, "finding all these . . . *maggots* for me to look after."

And with that cheerful introduction, our situation might have hit a new low. At the moment, I was actually more concerned about Wisty, whose eyes were scarily glazing over.

The Matron swiveled her chair away from us to grab a couple of thick files off the desk behind her. A greasy, heavy ponytail hung down the back of her white nurse's uniform like some enormous piece of seaweed or a dead lake eel.

"Yes, ma'am," said the guard. "'Maggots' is exactly right, only maybe a little too kind, if you ask me."

"I *didn't!*" snapped the Matron. The guard cowered and did his impression of a dashboard-mounted bobblehead in a dune buggy.

Then she heaved herself to her massive feet with a weary grunt. "You know why you're here, instead of some namby-pamby jail?" she asked.

"No, sir," I said, clearing my throat.

"Funny boy." Her eyes narrowed to gleaming slits. "This is a *dangerous* place," she said. "For *dangerous* criminals. But keep in mind that your cheap tricks won't work in here, my pretties!"

Did she actually just call us "my pretties"? Did I hear her right? Maybe there *was* a reason I was in a psychiatric hospital.

"The New Order's had this place spellproofed." She gloated, and then her expression changed and she began muttering to herself. "I don't know what they think I'm going to do with any more of this filth, though."

The Matron led us down the hallway to a thick wooden door with a wire-glassed window. She unlocked it, and the guards very roughly pushed us inside. They removed our chains and tossed our meager belongings—one drumstick and one empty book—on the floor behind us.

"Welcome to death row," she said as she slammed the door shut and locked us inside.

Chapter 23

Wisty

"A LITTLE CREEPY, huh?" I said, trying to make it sound like this place wasn't much worse than a haunted mansion at a kiddie theme park.

"Uh, not as creepy as *you*," said Whit. "I hate to break this to you, sis, but... um, you're glowing."

Glowing? Does not compute. *Does not compute.*

"Huh?" I said, deadpan. "What do you mean?"

"What part of 'you're glowing' do you not understand?" he asked.

"The part where I'm glowing," I said. "How could—"

I looked down and saw that my skin, my clothes, the air about an inch around my body, were suffused with a thin, faint, greenish light—enough to see by.

"Have you been playing in toxic waste lately?" Whit made an unfunny.

I held my shaking hand out and examined it. It started to get so bright I had to turn away. The whole room lit up—the dark, grime-filled crevices, the piles of medical waste, the bedpans, the holes in the baseboard that could easily accommodate rats.

"Ugh." Whit winced. "Do me a favor and hit the dimmer switch."

"I don't know if I can," I said, my voice cracking a little.

Except for my flighty flower-power first name, I'd mostly escaped freakishness in my life. Didn't have to wear hideous hand-me-down clothes from an older sister. Never the last one picked for a team in gym class. Never called four eyes, metal mouth, or fatty. Now I was an official freak, three times over. A witchy flamethrowing radioactive freak.

That's not great news for a fifteen-year-old, let me tell you.

I suddenly welled up with tears, desperately needing my parents. "Mom? Dad?" I whimpered. The echo of their names hit my ears cruelly.

Whit got that annoyingly worried look on his face again. "Wisty…"

"Shh," I hissed, crying now. "Mom…told me about *everything*, Whit. She told me about the birds and the bees, like, way before any of my other friends' parents did. How she and Dad fell in love—very romantic. And Dad—he told me about his most embarrassing moments in school. And how proud he was of you, and me, and…and he was never afraid to say 'I love you' like the other dads." I sucked in a tortured breath. "But *why* didn't they tell me about all of *this*?"

Whit came close and hugged me, glow and all.

"The worst thing is, Whit, maybe they *did* tell me about it. And maybe I just wasn't paying enough attention."

Then I really started sobbing. My tears soaked into Whit's jumpsuit, and he held me until we both sank into sleep, and my glow faded, faded away.

Chapter 24

Whit

WHOA!

Celia came to visit me again that night, or sometime during those first harried hours in the new jail. I wasn't so sure about the passage of time anymore. I wasn't sure about anything.

"Hi, Whit, missed you," Celia said, same as before, only now she said it with a wink. "I was thinking about you. The way it was. Happy days. Our first date. You wore that wrinkly bowling shirt you love. *Alley Cat*. Remember?"

Of course I remembered.

Oh man, oh man, oh Celia. What is happening? Am I totally insane? Is that why I'm in a nuthouse? "Celes, listen, I need to ask you a question. Why did you stay away for so long? Please, if you don't want me to go completely crazy, tell me what happened to you."

Amazingly—especially if this was a dream—Celia reached out and touched me. I could feel her. It made me calm. Calmer. She felt like the old Celia, looked like the old Celia . . . and had the same sweet smile.

"I *will* tell you what happened to me, Whit. I want to so badly."

"Thank you." I let out a sigh from the bottom of my sneakers. "Thank you."

"Not now, though. When I see you for real. In person. Not in a dream. We have to be careful, though — The One Who Is The One is watching us."

I couldn't let Celia go again. I held her close — very close — and I asked her once more for some kind of rational explanation.

Then Celia pulled away, but just far enough for her to stare into my eyes. I loved being able to look into her eyes again. We had the same baby blues. Her friends used to joke about the kids we'd have one day.

"Here's all I can tell you for now, Whit. There's a prophecy. It's written on a wall in your future. Learn about it. Never forget it. You're a part of it, of running the world. That's why the New Order's so afraid of you and Wisteria."

I couldn't even *absorb* that major information drop before she took a quick breath and continued. "Whit, I can't be here any longer than this. I love you. Please miss me."

"Don't go," I pleaded. "I can't take this again. *Celia?*"

She was gone, but somehow I could still hear her voice: "We'll be together again, Whit. I miss you already. Miss me. Please miss me."

Chapter 25

Wisty

THAT MORNING, Whit and I were startled awake by a tapping sound, like a stick or maybe somebody's cane. My heart immediately started racing full blast, but Whit still seemed groggy and disoriented.

"Celia," he mumbled. I shoved myself away from him. I loved my brother, but this was no time for hopeless romanticism.

"No, it's your sister, and as a reminder, we're at home sweet hellhouse," I said, and gave him a gentle slap. "Wake up! I need you here, dude!"

I held my breath as the knob slowly turned. By the time Whit showed any recognition of where he was, the door had opened several inches, but all I could see was the dimly lit hall through the crack.

A cold voice finally came from behind the door. "Thank you, Matron." Its evil chill made my heart practically stop. "I'll take it from here, if I may."

"Watch yourself, now," said the Matron. "These are dangerous fiends."

"Thank you for your concern, but I think I'll be just fine." The door opened wider, and a towering skeletal figure—almost inhumanly tall—stepped into our room.

He was like Death itself, but in modern garb. A charcoal suit hung on him as if he were made of clothes hangers. His skin had a ghastly pallor, unhealthy as a plant left in a closet. For years.

Instinctively I moved back. Then, like a snake striking, a black leather riding crop whipped through the air with a hiss and smacked me hard. "Hey!"

The sting was icy cold, then burning, and I gasped and clutched my hand to my chest.

"No, you don't, witch," the Death figure commanded. "Your days of controlling people and objects with your evil powers are over. *I* am here now. I am your *Visitor*."

Chapter 26

Whit

WHEN THAT BULLYING, cowardly freak smacked Wisty's hand with his snake whip, I almost lunged for him. I was ready to fight to the death, whatever it took. Nobody hits my sister.

Wisty bravely cradled her hand and watched him, her jaw set.

I glared at this Visitor creep, trying to distract him. "Let me guess. No one loved you as a child. Or as an adult. Well, tough noogies!"

Then, *smack!* I gasped as the riding crop whipped across my face, opening up my skin with a white-hot sting. Blood started running down my cheek.

"This is your first full day at the Hospital, wizard," said the Visitor. "So I'm going to be especially gentle with you. But you won't ever speak to the Matron or me that way again. We're the only things standing between you and a fate far worse than death."

"So there's something *worse* than being kidnapped in the middle of the night, kept in prison, sentenced to death in a laughable trial, and then locked up in a condemned hospital with two sadists? It's going to get *worse?!*"

"Are you done?" he asked calmly.

I shrugged and was just deciding what to say next when the crop zapped out of nowhere and hit me on the left ear, then the right ear, then the tip of my chin.

"Yessss. Much worse," said the Visitor. "Your file indicated you weren't the brightest bulb in the chandelier. At any rate, you would do well to learn this much: *this*"—he sighed and gestured around our dank and disgusting cell—"is your new home.

"We have armed guards, security cameras, electronic perimeters, and multiple lethal safeguards that I'm not at liberty to discuss. Also, you'll have no luck circumventing any of these systems with your trickery. This entire building has been altered to dampen your energies, and you will find you have no powers here. In short, once you walked in the door, you effectively became *normal.*"

Wisty and I exchanged a glance meaning "except for glowing." I swear we could read each other's mind sometimes, especially lately.

"As to this room's amenities, please note that your one external window has a western exposure, through which you can see the blackness of a ten-story-deep ventilation shaft, the bottom of which is fitted with a turbine that could grind a blue whale into mush in less than ten seconds. Feel free to throw yourselves down it at any time."

He continued like a hotel bellman describing an executive suite. "You also have your own semiprivate bathroom, complete with our special-issue toilet paper that feels so airy, you'll swear it's not even there."

I looked into our doorless bathroom nook, which contained a seatless toilet surrounded by dust and chunks of fallen plaster, and I confirmed that, yes, in fact, *there was no toilet paper.*

The Visitor looked down his long, hooked nose at us. "I will be back periodically to check on you," he said in his deep zombielike voice. "If you misbehave in any way, well"—he paused and gave a smile that would have made a crocodile look cheerful—"I will mete out punishment."

Sssst! The riding crop slashed through the air, missing my eye by a whisker. "I'll see you soon.... *Promise.*"

Then he was gone, and the lock turned behind him.

"I don't much care for him," said Wisty. "You?"

Chapter 27

Whit

WISTY THEN SUMMED UP our situation with typical offhanded precision.

"This totally sucks," she said.

I considered that. Between our various bruises, bumps, cuts, welts, and torn clothes, it looked like we'd been in a cage match with a wolverine.

I also had less than a month to live.

"Much too optimistic," I said. "You always see the bright side, don't you?"

I wandered around the room, trying to distract myself from the burning pain of my injuries. But I was having trouble forming thoughts... other than self-torturing ones about juicy burgers and black-and-white milk shakes... and cheese fries. I'd never been so hungry in all my life.

Then I noticed Wisty sitting on the mattress, moving her lips silently.

"Talking to yourself already?" I asked.

"Why not? We're in an insane asylum." She smiled, then looked a little bit sheepish. "Actually, if you need to know, I'm trying to come up with a spell. You know, to get us out of here. If I'm a witch, I ought to be able to go 'shazam' and blast the door open."

"They said we had no power here. You weren't paying attention to The One With The Bullwhip."

"Really? Then tell me that my little radioactive moment was just a weird dream," she said.

"Okay, you win, glowgirl," I said. "So, you think 'shazam' will do it? Go for it."

She waved her hands at the door. *"Shazam!"* she yelled.

Snick! It popped right open.

Chapter 28

Whit

"HERE. BOTH OF YOU!" The Matron's bigfoot-size body filled our doorway. "Come with me, vermin. I suppose it's time you learned how to get food and water."

In the woman's massive hands were two beat-up plastic pails, which she flung out to us. Call it a hunch, but this already didn't look good. I'd have done anything to get a drink of water, though. The sink in our bathroom didn't work...and what was in the toilet wasn't exactly, um, potable.

We each took a pail and followed the Matron as she noisily clomped down the dark hall, her keys jangling with each lurching step and her preternaturally huge feet sausaged into chunky white shoes.

I started to make out noises ahead, and they were vaguely...animalish. Snarls, growls, and high-pitched whines filled my ears.

"What is this?" Wisty croaked. "Now what?"

The Matron gestured toward the end of the hall. "There's food way, way, *way* down there. And water. Use your pails." She looked down at her enormous steel-banded watch. "You have four minutes. If you're not back by then"—her black eyes shone and her mouth stretched in a horrible approximation of a smile—"then I'll know you've passed to the other side. Violently."

Turning, she clomped her way back to the nurses' station fifty yards behind us. "Take care," she called.

My palm was already sweaty where I held on to the thin metal handle of my pail. The hallway in front of us was lined on either side by . . . canine animals of some sort. Mad dogs? Wolves? Black-furred hyenas? Hungry, angry, hostile animals, chained to the walls up and down the hallway.

Somehow we had to get past them—and back—in four minutes . . . but only if we wanted food and water.

Only if we wanted to live.

Chapter 29

Wisty

ANYONE WHO'S EVER BEEN on the verge of a major disaster, possibly even death, will tell you that the most mundane things can go through your mind. Just before I was about to sacrifice my life to the animals, I thought about a really mean dog that used to live on our block. When I was little, my friends and I always rode our bikes on the other side of the street, because the dog looked wild and we were scared it would break free and bite our butts.

Her name was Princess. She was a shih tzu. And she now seemed like a fuzzy teddy bear that I could have dressed up in doll clothes for a tea party.

"Are those *dogs?*" Whit asked hoarsely as we started down the hallway. "Or wolves?"

I shook my head. "I'm going with hellhounds."

"Do you think maybe you could burst into flames again?" Whit whispered.

"I can't do it on purpose," I croaked, frustrated. "I'm trying. Not happening."

"Okay. Well, I'll go," Whit rasped back, then blew out a thin gust of air.

"No," I wheezed. "I'm small and fast."

Before Whit and I had a chance to finish the argument, we saw a small, indistinct figure appear at the end of the hall. Holding a pail.

"Who's that?" I muttered.

Whoever it was suddenly darted forward, leaping and dodging and almost crashing against the wall, hurtling toward us at a furious pace. "It" was about thirty feet away when it suddenly tripped and fell.

Instantly several hounds fell on it, snarling and snapping. Just watching the awful scene took my breath away.

"I have to help," Whit said, making a move toward the hapless soul.

But then the little figure bounced up, pail in hand, and hustled straight toward us again. I couldn't tell if it was a boy or a girl, but it was definitely a little kid, maybe five or six years younger than me. Blood streaked the poor tyke's hair and ragged T-shirt. We stood to one side as he or she dashed past, then collapsed on the dirty floor, huddling against the wall, head and shoulders shaking.

The pail, which had fallen over when the child had tripped, was now completely empty. The hellhounds had eaten or drunk everything the kid had risked life and limb for.

Crying silently, the huddled figure grabbed the empty pail, skittered away on hands and knees to a couple of doors down the hall, and disappeared inside.

Whit and I looked on in shocked silence.

The Matron merely peered at her watch. "Seventy seconds," she told us. "*Ticktock*."

Chapter 30

Whit

HAVE YOU EVER TRIED to *think loudly*? It seems like a contradiction in terms. But you do what you gotta do when you have to pretend you can't hear the sounds of vicious snarling and snapping jaws and teeth all around you.

I had to shout in my head over and over as I bolted down the hall with both our pails, *Make like you're doing the hundred-yard dash—at the regional championship. Run, run, run!*

Argh! I felt my feet stumble but caught myself and kept sprinting. *Not the regional championship,* I thought. *The world championship.*

"Victory, victory, victory!" I yelled senselessly, hoping I never had to explain to Wisty that this was what I occasionally chanted to myself when I was in competition, to psych myself up, to help me pretend to be the all-American boy I thought everybody wanted me to be.

It sounded pretty lame in the middle of an obstacle

course of mad dogs, but it was working. Somehow I made it to the end of the hall with only a nip or two. I turned, gave Wisty a psychotic thumbs-up, then plowed through a doorway.

And stopped dead in my tracks.

It was pretty dark. And the room seemed empty. Was this the Matron's idea of a trap? Good one, if it was. Way to go, Matron.

For a second I felt more vulnerable than ever before. I half expected a mad dog or wolf to shoot out of the dark and tear into my face.

It seemed like an eternity before my eyes adjusted, but I finally detected two troughlike shapes against a wall. The Matron hadn't lied after all—amazing! I dashed over to them, sloppily filling my pails with sludgelike gruel and tepid water.

I was feeling so good, I dunked my face in the brackish liquid for a hearty slurp. The sensation of my head underwater gave me a rush of energy.

Clutching the pails to my chest, I sprinted out of the room, then down the hall toward my sister, who was jumping up and down like a manic cheerleader.

"Good hellhounds!" I heard her yell through the din of the barking devil dogs. "Sweet little hellhounds, let him through. Go, Whit, go!"

At that very moment, I felt the clamp of an animal's jaws on my pants.

I crashed against a wall, but I kept my focus—*Victory,*

victory, victory! — and surged forward through the growls and snarls.

Seeing Wisty's face ahead supercharged me for the last few paces. I practically flew into her arms, and she hugged me hard.

"You're awesome!" she gushed. "You did great, Whit."

The Matron was striding toward us, holding her stun gun at eye level. "Foul!" she called out. *Foul?* Without warning, she hit me with a jolt.

I barely knew what had happened as I collapsed and the pails tumbled and rolled.

"Four minutes, six seconds!" the Matron shrieked. "No food. No water!"

She snatched the pails away as I drooled on the floor.

Chapter 31

Whit

AS THE DAYS PASSED, my sister and I managed to stave off death by dehydration by locating a drip of what we hoped was rainwater or condensation just outside our ventilation-shaft window. By snaking a piece of wire for it to run along and then planting at the other end a crumpled paper cup we'd found, we got a few mouthfuls every three or four hours. It tasted like drywall dust, but it was a total lifesaver.

The whole thing was so backward. Last week a bad day was getting busted for exercising my right not to do trigonometry homework and having to face two hours after school with some of my best friends in detention.

This week, if only from the sheer boredom and depression of this place, I would have faced my trig textbook like it was *The Ultimate Book of Hot Cars*.

Then one afternoon, I was lying on our mattress and thinking about Celia, hoping she would come back, even in another dream, when my sister exclaimed, "Whit! Whit! WHIT! Will you look at me, please? WHITFORD!"

Wisty's voice brought me back to the totally screwed-up here and now. I kept my eyes closed, wanting to sink right back into my Celia thoughts.

"*Whit!*" Her stupid drumstick whacked my leg. "Open your eyes right now!"

"Ow! *What* is so important?" I griped, sitting up and snatching away the drumstick with irritation. "The pizza's here?"

My sister stood in front of me, holding out the journal. "*Look* at this!" she said, shaking the dusty book in my face.

I took the tome and examined the cover. Seemed the same to me.

"So what? It's old, it's musty, it's useless."

"Flip through the pages. Do it, Whit. Humor me."

Then I saw the impossible. Suddenly the journal was filled with words, pictures, illustrations. And handwriting that looked like my father's.

"Holy—" I stood up. "It's the next book in the Percival Johnson series. That's not supposed to come out until next year," I said. "That's interesting. *The Thunder Stealer* was one of my all-time favorite books."

"*What?*" Wisty said. "Are you seeing the same thing I am?"

I turned pages. "Holy crap." I thumbed forward. "*The Ultimate Book of Hot Cars!*"

"Hold on. I didn't see that!" Wisty snatched the book

back. "No, no, it's got the *History of World Art*! And prints by my favorite artists, Pepe Pompano and Margie O'Greeffe. And it's got all my favorite novels too!" She quickly riffled through the pages. "See?" She held the journal under my nose, its pages open. "Look, everything by my favorite writer, K. J. Meyers. And it's got *The Blueprints of Bruno Genet*. And *The Firegirl Saga*. Right here!"

I looked. This time I saw *The Swimsuit Issue Deluxe Compendium*.

"Whit...I think I get it," Wisty said with a hushed kind of awe. "The book shows each of us what we want to see." Then her eyes got huge and she stared at me. "It's magic. That's why Dad gave it to you."

I took the journal back from Wisty. "Show me where Celia is," I tried halfheartedly, but then actually held my breath like I was expecting something.

Nothing. Unless *The Ultimate Book of Hot Cars* was supposed to somehow take me to Celia.

"We have to figure out how all this works," Wisty said tensely. "I know you think I'm crazy, but I'm starting to really believe in us. Our magic. We just have to practice, Whit. We have to work harder. Maybe you *are* a wizard. Maybe I *am* a witch."

Chapter 32

Wisty

I HAD A REALLY GREAT TEACHER ONCE, Mrs. Solie, who told us she had the one true secret to happiness. She said it was all about seeing life as half full instead of half empty, no matter what happened to you. Actually, I was pretty okay with that. But what about when it's .000001 full?

The days passed—and there were tests, tests, TESTS. Medical tests, physical-strength tests, intelligence tests, "normality" tests, patriotism tests, more medical tests.

One particular night, when I was barely awake and suffering absolutely horrendous hunger pains, they grabbed Whit from our cell and took him away.

"You can't!" I screamed. "It's not his time yet! I've been counting! It's not time! He's not eighteen!"

But the next thing I knew, the Matron was dragging me out of the room too, then pushing me down a long hall to a lone window.

She pointed outside, to a cement courtyard below. She was singsonging under her foul breath, "Happy birthday to you, happy birthday to you, happy birthday, dear Whit...happy *death* day to you."

My blood froze and my heart nearly stopped beating. In the courtyard was an old-fashioned gallows.

She continued into the second verse: "How dead are you now? How dead are you now?" and then broke into a hideous donkey bray.

A few seconds later, a troop of guards pushed Whit ahead of them out into the courtyard. His hands and feet were in cuffs, which made him stumble-walk.

I tried to swallow but couldn't as I watched a guard put a black hood over Whit's head.

"No!" I shouted, pounding my fists against the glass. "No!" I pounded again, and blinked, and then suddenly...

I was falling.

Chapter 33

Wisty

THUNK! GASPING AND BLINKING, I looked around the claustrophobic jail cell, adrenaline already zapping my brain awake.

I saw Whit blinking in sleepy surprise. Then he sat up and stared hard at me. At that moment I realized my butt and back were aching, and it all came together.

I had been floating in my sleep. The nightmare about the gallows had woken me up, and I had woken...in *midair.*

Unfortunately, my bony little butt was not designed for crashing into a hard floor from a height of, oh, maybe four feet?

"Uh, Wisty," Whit said, "you were floating. Up in the air."

I just looked at him, so, so happy that he was alive, and *here,* not hanged.

Still shaken from the horrible dream, I felt cold sweat drying on the back of my neck. I looked above me as if I might see the wires and pulleys that had made it possible for me to float. There was nothing.

"Floating," repeated Whit, sounding amazed, "in your sleep. And they think we don't have any special powers in here."

I wanted to deny it, but here I was, with a sore backside, and I had definitely felt myself dropping through the air. I got to my feet, standing in the space I'd been, um, floating in.

Experimentally, I waved my useless drumstick around. Nothing happened.

"My sister, the witch." Whit laughed. "Why can't you conjure up a double cheeseburger or something useful? A jumbo ice-cream sundae? A *stun gun*?"

I sighed and went to sit next to him on the mattress. "You're laughing, Whit, but . . . this whole witch-and-wizard thing. The flames. The glowing. The gavel-stopping. Now the floating. I think we really are . . . magic."

It felt like I was saying, "I guess I really *am* a supermodel."

"That's right, Detective Allgood," Whit said. "And now we have to figure out how to focus our inner sorcerers to get us out of this dump."

"Okay," I said, tapping my drumstick gently on the floor. It was only a stupid drumstick, but I'd found that I felt better with it in my hand—maybe it helped me think, or something spirity like that.

"I could flame out and set the Matron on fire," I suggested. "If I could figure out how to do it on purpose."

"Great. And then we'll have a burned-up giantess on our hands, plus a bunch of angry guards," said Whit.

"Right. Maybe I could float out the air shaft," I said, looking at the tiny, dark window above my head, then picturing myself dropping down it, many floors to the bottom, and getting pulverized by the turbine below.

"Maybe we can snap our fingers and a golden staircase will appear out of nowhere with angels singing and pointing the way to escape," Whit said glumly. "Or maybe we'll just grow wings and fly out of here."

I snorted. "Yeah. Kids with wings. That's likely."

Wham!

Whit and I jumped about a foot in the air, then whirled toward the door. It had swung open and smacked the wall like a hard kick. We waited, both of us as tight as coiled springs.

One thing we'd learned: anything that came through that door wasn't good.

Chapter 34

Wisty

"BREAKFAST IS SERVED! Poached eggs with bacon, fresh fruit, waffles, and syrup. Just *kidding,* kiddies."

The Visitor appeared, dressed in black again, his icy green eyes glittering as if he had a fever. I thought that if he looked at me long enough, the blood would start to freeze in my veins.

He stepped farther into the room, examining everything like he was some anal-retentive crime-scene investigator, tapping on the walls, testing the strength of the wire-glassed window in the door.

"Keeping you here is a waste of time, space, and money," he muttered, not bothering to look at us. "Waiting until you're eighteen is arbitrary. You're a drain on the taxpayers' money...feeding you, housing you."

"Um, I'm no economics expert, sir," Whit said with a smile so fake it made *my* teeth hurt, "but even I know that it's not costing the taxpayers more than a dime a day to keep us here."

The Visitor glared at us from the entryway to the bathroom. "I thought that you'd learned not to talk back to me, idiot." He reached into his suit pocket and pulled out an ancient toothbrush. "As punishment, you will scrub your bathroom with this cleaning utensil. When I return, it better be operating-room hygienic." The Visitor wrote something down on a clipboard. "There's no place in the New Order for your kind," he muttered.

"Excuse me, sir"—I finally spoke up—"but what exactly is the New Order?"

The Visitor wheeled and stared at me. His black riding crop dangled menacingly from one arm.

Then he began to speak—all singsongy: "The New Order is a bright new future. It is a future that replaces the corrupting and illusory freedoms of so-called democracies and replaces them with a higher discipline. It has taken many, many years of planning, strategic political postings, scientific polling, demographic research, precise messaging, and carefully monitored elections.

"For this rare moment in human history, those who have values and principles are in a position to do what is best. And part of what is best, of course, is taking steps to eliminate the deviants, the criminals, and all those who threaten prosperity and the New Order way."

He smoothed a hand over his slicked-back hair. "Like you two."

"But...what's *wrong* with us, sir?" I asked like I was the resident classroom dunce.

The Visitor's icy eyes narrowed, and he stepped closer until I could faintly smell mothballs and hair syrup.

"You *know* what's wrong with you. You're a virus," he hissed. "You two are the worst kind of deviants. Performance artists. Illusionists."

My jaw almost dropped. "But we're just kids!"

"Kids," he spat, as if he were saying "pus-filled blister." "Many, many, *many* children are unacceptable in the New Order."

Right then I should have shut up, wiped my face clear of any expression, and stood quietly till he was gone.

Instead, I stamped my foot. "We. Are. Just. *Kids!*"

The last word was practically a shriek, and as the Visitor raised his riding crop over his head, a maniacal look of delight on his face . . .

Whoosh! I was aflame for the first time since we'd gotten to Camp Alcatraz. Big flames. Impressive, even to a fire starter like me.

Whit cheered. "Thatagirl!"

Through the veil of dancing flames, I saw the Visitor staring at me in horror, backing away hurriedly toward the door. I opened my arms and stalked him like a zombie. "How 'bout a hug, big fella?"

"Freak!" the Visitor yelled just before he slammed the door to our cell.

"Way to prove we're just kids, inferno girl," Whit said. "But very cool anyway."

Chapter 35

Wisty

I DIPPED THE TOOTHBRUSH in the gray-watered toilet and scrubbed another inch of floor. I was singing as if I had lost my mind, and probably I had.

"I've been working on the railroad, all the livelong day."

By this time I'd been through every single *good* song I could remember the lyrics to—and believe me, there are a *lot*—and now I was at the very bottom of the barrel, reaching back to preschool days. I used to be the ultimate karaoke queen, because I grew up with my parents always playing all kinds of music at our house: old stuff, new stuff, classical, blues, jazz, rock, pop, and, yeah, even hiphop. I'm talking everything from Toasterface to Ron Sayer to Lay-Z.

That's how freaking cool my parents were. I mean, *are*.

That fleeting bittersweet thought of my mom and dad got me out of the scrubbing groove, and I had to belt out the song even louder to reboot. Clearly, Whit wasn't interested in listening.

"So, the Visitor seems afraid of fire," Whit said, leaning against the wall for a work break.

"Yeah, Whitford, *most* people don't freak out when somebody suddenly bursts into flames," I said, rolling my eyes. "What a wuss that Visitor is."

"We're a witch and a wizard. What does that even *mean?*" Whit continued. "It's been a long time since I've read any fairy tales. I couldn't even tell you what witches and wizards are supposed to do...except—shouldn't we at least be able to do things *on purpose,* instead of all this stuff we have no control over?"

"I know. If I had a dime for every *'alakazam'* I've done where nothing happened, I'd be able to buy a brand-new wardrobe. With a cute purse-size dog to match every outfit." I paused, my arm aching. "Wait. I take that back. I don't even *want* that. I want—"

Whit interrupted my reverie. "There has to be a point—"

His voice was clipped by a strangled gulp. I jumped to my feet. Whit was staring at his arm.

So was I.

His hand had sunk right into the wall.

Not "sunk" like he'd busted his fist right through the cement. More "sunk" like, I don't know, the molecules that made up the wall had rearranged themselves around his hand.

"Um, can you take your hand *out?*" I asked. "Please try."

A concerned look crossed my brother's face, but he removed his hand without any obvious pain or resistance. We both examined it: same old hand. Then he put it against the wall and gently pushed again. The hand sank in several inches, its outline blurring beneath the wall molecules.

"I can only go in up to my elbow," he reported. "After that, the wall sort of firms up again."

I shook my head. "Totally bizarre. But useful? Not so much. Not unless you can go all the way through. For God's sake, don't put your head in there," I said.

Whit's muffled voice came next.

He had stuck his head in the wall.

"You won't believe this!" His words were garbled. "Total mindblower."

Chapter 36

Whit

I BLINKED—YOU KNOW, like, whoever blinks first loses.

I could see...a total shadow world. It looked like a whole other dimension, another reality. Everything was black, or gray, or tinged with glowy green. I could make out fuzzy shapes moving and staticky snippets of distorted conversation.

It was kind of like watching a horror movie on an old TV with incredibly bad reception.

Wisty had started pulling on my shirt from the other side of the wall. I could barely hear her voice, which freaked me out in itself.

Some of the shadows were getting clearer—because they were coming closer, which I didn't particularly appreciate so much.

"Just stay where you are," I tried to say, but my voice was lost. Then one of the shadow people turned toward me anyway, like it could hear.

It sure looked like a human form. Then the mouth opened—nothing but a shapeless splotch in a dark shadow world. If the figure was saying something, I couldn't understand.

Slowly, it approached—cautiously. Then I distinctly heard the words "Is someone there?"

As I watched in awed silence, the shadow's face became clearer, more detailed—until I screamed.

It was Celia.

And this time it wasn't a dream.

Chapter 37

Whit

"CELIA!" I CALLED OUT, but my throat felt raw and my voice seemed to get snatched away from me again, not to mention that my knees had begun to knock.

Celia froze, looking all around, like she didn't see me standing right there a few feet away from her.

"Celia! It's me, Whit. I can see you. I'm here. *Wherever this is.*"

Suddenly her eyes locked on mine. She blinked. Blinked a second time. Then she stepped back in surprise.

"It's me. I'm really here. You said we'd meet again. For real."

On the other side, Wisty was still calling my name, yelling for me to come back. But I couldn't tear my eyes away from Celia. Her skin seemed even paler than in my dreams. But her eyes still shone, spoke the truth to me, and she was as beautiful as ever, maybe even more beautiful. She had this inner light.

"Whit?" She licked her lips—a familiar nervous habit of hers—and finally came closer. "Whit, I can see you now. How did you—where are you?"

"Believe it or not, I'm in the bathroom of a cell in a mental hospital," I said, my words spinning away from me. I felt like I had to reach out to her. Maybe I could pull Celia back with me. "But where are you?"

Celia gave me the oddest look, and a cold hand grabbed at my heart.

"Whit," she whispered urgently, "you have to go right now. You shouldn't be here. It's dangerous!"

"Why?!" I burst out.

"I'm sorry," Celia began, "but I have to tell you what really happened to me." Then her voice broke, and she started to cry. "They murdered me. They said...it was because of you and your sister. It happened at the Hospital, Whit. The New Order and The One Who Is The One—he's behind this. He's so awful, so powerful."

I was crying now too. My body was shaking and numb at the extremities. "I see you. You said we'd meet. And you're here with me. *You're not dead, Celia.*"

"Don't come here again, Whit," she warned. "This is the Shadowland. It's a place for spirits. That's what I am now. I'm a ghost."

Chapter 38

Whit

"WHIT, COME BACK here this second! *Whitford!*"

Suddenly I felt Wisty's wiry arms loop really tight around my waist. "Wisty, no!" I tried to push her off, but she'd always been like a limpet, able to cling, and strong. I could feel her brace her feet against the wall, and then she pulled as hard as she could, even as I fought against her.

Either I wasn't as strong as I used to be, or Wisty was stronger than ever. She yanked me out of the wall, away from Celia, and we both flew across the room. We hit hard against the opposite wall.

We got ourselves untangled, but I rushed back to the wall like somebody possessed.

"Whit, no!" Wisty yelled. *"NO! No, Whit. Please."*

"Celia!" I screamed, my lips pressed against the cool surface. "Come back!" I pushed at the wall. Pounded it. Tried to put my fist through it. I couldn't get inside again. Finally I gave up and broke down.

Wisty just stared at me, with both hands clasped on top of her head. She had every reason to believe that I'd gone over the edge for good.

"Wisty, I saw Celia."

"What?" She stared blankly. "In the *wall?*"

I told her everything that I'd seen, everything Celia said. How she'd been killed because of us. How she was a ghost now.

Wisty was speechless as she tried to process the next unbelievable twist in our lives: *I had seen and talked to a ghost.*

Then I heard the sound of the door to our cell being unlocked.

Chapter 39

Wisty

THE MATRON BARGED IN and informed us we were going back to see Judge Ezekiel Unger, of all people. Maybe there had been a mistake, and we weren't the witch and wizard? Or our parents had interceded somehow? Whatever it was, something major had happened. Maybe we were going to get a sliver of our humanity back.

After a not-so-tender good-bye from the Matron came a fast ride in a grungy van that had the coppery smell of blood, and maybe the scent of something that very scared animals do.

"You're shivering," said Whit. He gently kissed the top of my head. The fact is that we had always loved each other, but we'd quarreled over the most petty and ridiculous things. No more. *Life,* as the wiser-than-you-might-think saying goes, *is too short.* Plus, it seemed so obvious to me now: Whit was a great brother. I wished that it wouldn't have taken a New Order hellhole to prove that one to me.

The van screeched to a stop, and we were yanked outside. We entered a tall building and were suddenly surrounded by stark, monochromatic New Order normalcy: bright lights, a court hallway, regular-looking New Order people wearing neat, boring New Order clothes, cell phones ringing with the same preprogrammed, single-note tones. Pictures of The One Who Is The One were everywhere. And black-on-red N.O. signs were on all the walls. It made our prison days and nights seem just a little more bearable. At least we'd been missing *this* crap.

Whit put his face close to mine, and he whispered, "If we get a chance, we run! We join hands and run. And don't look back, no matter what."

A guard threw open an ornately carved door, and...

We were back in that awful courtroom. And there was Judge Ezekiel Unger, looking like Death's first and favorite cousin.

"The One Who Judges!" announced a simpering New Order lackey.

As if maybe we'd forgotten what the big creep looked like.

This time there was no hating jury, no mocking audience. Just The One Who Judges, the armed guards, and...*the Visitor.* I groaned to myself when I saw him. He'd probably brought us up on charges for improper toilet cleaning, or pail spilling in the Hallway of Mad Dogs.

Judge Unger was reading a thick report, sparing only a quick, disgusted glance at us before turning another page and reading on.

"Wisteria Allgood," the judge said at last, raising his lifeless eyes to me. "Whitford Allgood." Somehow, he managed to make the word "good" in our names sound like evil itself. "I trust you're enjoying your stay at the Hospital?"

"Fantastic!" I said — couldn't resist. "Five stars."

"I have here your medical reports," he went on, ignoring me completely, waving the thick document as if it weighed nothing at all. His eyes were lasered on us. "Your tests have come back... *normal*. Every single test!"

My heart gave a little leap. Thank God! This had all been a terrible, terrible mistake. Now we would be returned to our parents and go home. The nightmare was finally over.

"I want to know right this instant," the judge continued, "whom you bribed. Was it him? Was it the Visitor? I suspect it was him."

Chapter 40

Wisty

"BRIBED?" WHIT CHOKED OUT, and I thought the top of his head might blow off and start spinning around. At this point I could say honestly, *stranger things have happened.*

"The Visitor?!" I said. "You've got nothing to fear there — trust me, he's a loyal and worthy sadist."

"Of course you bribed someone!" the judge yelled. "*Normal?* You're the farthest thing from normal there is! Depraved is not normal. Deceitful is not normal. Dangerous to society is not normal."

Whit was very close to the edge. "And completely *insane* is not normal either! What could we bribe anyone *with?* Gruel? Mice droppings? Beauty tips from that freaky Matron?"

Judge Unger's face flushed almost purple with fury. "You don't ask the questions, pretty boy," he said, spewing wrath the way Italian fountains spurt water. "You answer the questions! Now, for the last time, *who was it?* I know it wasn't the Matron. She's my beloved sister."

There's a shocker, I thought wearily, and made a mental note not to make any more Matron jokes today.

"And," he continued, "if you say another word against her, I will hold you in contempt of court. The penalty for which will make all the rest of this look like kindergarten."

You're a lowly, miserable cock-a-roach, I thought.

Meanwhile, Whit retorted, "I'm sorry. Maybe your little lackeys' test machines weren't working properly that day?"

"Shut up!" screamed the judge. "You obviously did something to the testing apparatuses. You used your wizardry on them! You fixed the results!"

Roach! You're a roach! I shouted inside my head. *If only I could turn Judge Unger into a roach,* I thought. *I'm a witch, right? Why can't I do this? Why, why, why?*

Turn into a roach, I murmured silently. *Turn into a roach!*

My brain began to ache with the effort. Witches cast spells. I didn't know any spells. I remembered only a few rhymes from when I was a kid. Did I know any rhymes about roaches?

The only chant thingy I could think of was

Flies in the kitchen, lawsy, mawsy,
  Flies in the night, lawsy may
Flies on the river, lawsy, mawsy
  Flies at first light, lawsy may.

And who knew what the heck *that* meant?

The judge was still screaming at Whit, and Whit's face was stiff—he was trying so hard not to lose his temper. A sister recognizes the signs.

Suddenly a loud buzzing distracted me, and I looked away from Whit to the air above me.

Could it be possible?

The sound became louder, and then one of the guards said, "What the—? Hey! My God, my Lord, my Good God!"

The courtroom was suddenly full of enormous biting horseflies.

I'd brought on a plague.

Chapter 41

Wisty

HORSEFLIES. They were dive-bombing everywhere I looked—crazed rogues, intent on sucking our blood. I had created them. *Total, total oops.*

If someone had tossed a sackful of stink bombs and some M-80s into the courtroom right then, it couldn't have caused a bigger commotion. Tough-guy guards were frantically waving their arms over their heads and screaming like little boys who'd stumbled into a hornet's nest.

Judge Unger's jaw dropped in stunned horror. He quickly shut it when several humongous flies attempted kamikaze missions down his throat.

Whit and I ducked under a table. "What's going on?!" he said. "Did you—"

"Um," I began guiltily, "sort of. Maybe. Yes."

"Wisty, what did you do?" Whit whispered against my ear.

"I don't know exactly what I did," I answered. "There was a song about flies, and flies on the river, and lawsy, mawsy."

The buzzing quieted suddenly. *That's it?* I thought. *That's the whole plague?*

Chapter 42

Wisty

I PEERED OUT from beneath the table and saw the Visitor whirling this way and that, helplessly swatting at the air with his sticklike arms. Judge Unger was peeking out from beneath his tent of robes, his eyes the size of baseballs.

Then, "Oh God!" one of the guards screamed.

"God, no!" yelled another. "This is worse! *Much* worse!"

I couldn't believe what I saw now. All the flies were gone. But stuck to everybody's arms and faces—to any bare skin at all—were...small, dark splotches.

That *moved!*

"Oh man," Whit breathed. "The flies all turned into *leeches!*"

"I didn't say anything about leeches," I said in a defensive whisper.

Apparently those nasty little suckers were elastic as all get-out. One guard tried to pull a bug off his lip, and it stretched and stretched until it broke in a disgusting yellowish mess. More leeches clung to walls, desks, and chairs—thousands of them, moving around like giant blood-seeking clingworms. Some were dropping from the ceiling.

"This is probably the most repulsive thing I've ever seen," Whit said. "Even given what we've been through at the Hospital. I kind of like it."

"Hey," I said, "in case you haven't noticed, they don't seem to be crawling all over *us*."

Then a booming voice took over the courtroom.

"*Stop! Stop this kindergarten nonsense!* No more flies, no more leeches, no more uncivil disturbances of any kind."

Suddenly I felt weak in the knees, numb—paralyzed, actually. I remembered the feeling—how could I forget?

He was there, he'd just appeared, and he'd already ruined everything. The stuffy decorum, the New Order, the boring sameness... it was all back in place.

"I am The One Who Is The One. Just in case you forgot or possibly repressed the memory."

He strode forward until he was right on top of Whit and me.

"I have been observing you: here in the court, back at the Hospital. You see, youngins, I am everywhere, and obviously I am all-powerful, and you are not!"

He looked at Whit and actually gave a wink. "I can even shut *your sister* up. So who can doubt my power? Now... there will be more tests, tests, tests, *tests*. Until we find the answer I'm looking for, until we solve the puzzle of the Allgoods. I want to know about their power! Anti-gravity? Healing? Immortality? Physical transformation? Telekinesis?

"Take the prisoners back to the Hospital! And no more Mister Nice Guy tactics. Double their workload, double the tests, double the discomfort. I want *answers!*"

Finally his Oneness bent toward me, stopping just inches from my chin.

"*Witcheria,* is there anything you would like to say? Anything at all? Perhaps you're offended by the phrase 'kindergarten nonsense,' which I used to describe your paltry tricks here today? Well, you know the famous saying—of course you do—'TRICKS' ARE FOR KIDS! Get them both out of my sight!"

And then, I swear this is true, it was like a category-five hurricane was in that courtroom—and then The One Who Is The One was gone.

With the wind?

Chapter 43

Wisty

WHAT IS THAT dumb saying? *What doesn't kill you only makes you stronger.* Well, maybe there was some truth there. I definitely felt stronger, and angrier. I was burning up inside.

When we were returned to our cell in the Hospital, I was expecting the Matron to rush in and stun-gun us till we screamed for mercy. I was expecting the Visitor to come whip us to shreds with his riding crop. I was expecting them to throw us to the hellhounds for *their* supper.

Instead, it got a little worse than that.

They sent...Byron Swain.

Byron Snotty Traitor Suck-up Quisling Hall Monitor Swain. I wished we were back at our school, so Whit could have pounded him into the dust.

"Hail, prisoners," Byron said in that snide, nasal voice that could make a statue of Jesus roll its eyes in disgust.

"What do you want? Just couldn't stay away?" I asked. "Or are you a little Visitor-in-training?"

"So, we meet again," said Byron. Like before, he looked freshly dipped in antiseptic. His brown hair was just so, his eyes cold, perfect marbles. His chinos had a sharp crease down each leg.

My eyebrows rose. "That's the best you could come up with? 'We meet again'? I mean, cliché much?"

When I'd first arrived at the Hospital for the Supposedly Deranged, I'd been a scared, freaked-out kid. Now I felt like the freak-out bar had been raised pretty high. I wasn't going to let Ferret Face get me down.

Byron flushed and pressed his lips tightly together. "Shut up, witch!" he snapped. "Or I'll tell the Matron to stun-gun you till you have no more attitude than a head of lettuce."

Byron gave me a sardonic smile that I was sure he had practiced in a mirror, probably right after one of his sterile baths. "Now hear this. You have both been designated *Extremely Dangerous,* which is how the New Order characterizes the most severe threats and worst enemies."

"Extremely Dangerous," Whit said. "We're honored. We'd like to thank our parents, of course. And Coach Schwietzer at the high school."

Byron, or the Tattling Weasel, as I decided he should henceforth be known, went on. "As it happens, it turns out to be both good news and bad news for you. The good news is that you get a pass on all of those tests you heard about at trial. And the bad news? Well, a rating of Extremely Dangerous lowers the age for execution from eighteen down to...zero. Which means, let me see...both of you can now be executed...*tomorrow*."

He smirked and smoothed his presmoothed hair. "What's that you say? Black cat got your tongue? No wizardly wisecracks? Honestly, I'd love to know—what do you think of that hot pooping scoop?"

Chapter 44

Wisty

WELL, AT LEAST *SOMEBODY* on this lockstep planet was happy and excited.

But the Tattling Weasel's snotty smile had pushed me over the edge. And Whit was right there with me.

"You think that's funny?" my bro said in a low voice, his fists clenched. "What if Wisty were *your* sister, and she was going to be executed tomorrow?"

The Tattling Weasel looked at us smugly. "My sister was a traitor to the New Order." He spoke slowly to drive home the point. "And...I...turned her...*in*."

I couldn't believe it. Even back when Whit had drawn mustaches on every doll I had, and I had truly wished he'd never been born, at least I knew I wouldn't want him condemned to death. Torture, sure—but not death.

"So you think we're Extremely Dangerous?" I said, tapping my drumstick against my side.

"Yes," said the TW. "The world will be a far better place without either of you."

"Because I'm a scary witch?" I sneered. "A *bad*, scary witch?"

"That is correct," said the TW. "You probably sold your soul for your demonic powers."

I waved the drumstick at him. I saw fear and pride have a wrestling match on his little pointy face. He glared back at me. "Put that down. I command it!"

"Ooh, I'm a bad, scary witch," I said in a psycho kind of voice. "I'm going to turn you into a pumpkin! Bibbidi-Bobbidi-Boo!"

Then I brandished my drumstick as if it were actually a magic wand.

To my complete and utter astonishment, we heard a real live *crack* of electricity, and actual sparks flew out of the end of the stick. The TW gave a startled cry, and then there was a *boom* like a jet had just broken the sound barrier.

When the smoke in the room cleared, Whit and I were standing there, looking at...well, an honest mistake.

But a very bad mistake all the same.

Chapter 45

Wisty

I COULD HAVE SWORN I said "pumpkin." Didn't I say "pumpkin"?

"Um, I think I just turned the Tattling Weasel into a lion," I said weakly.

"That seems fairly obvious" was all Whit could say.

The lion coughed, putting one paw on its chest. "Ahem," it *spoke* in a scratchy voice. Then the very large cat opened its mouth wider and tried a practice roar.

"Change him back," Whit said as he pulled us up against the nearest wall. "Do it now! Quick, quick, quick! Before the weasel realizes he's changed into a man-eating carnivore! Try saying something other than 'pumpkin'!"

The lion roared again—even louder. It seemed to be warming up to the idea of being a lion. Then it sort of smiled at me. Mostly what I saw, though, were really long, sharp teeth.

"Change him *back*," Whit repeated, not taking his eyes off the king of beasts.

The lion opened its mouth again and let out a huge roar. It blew my hair back, filling the room and reverberating off the walls.

I raised my drumstick. "Bibbidi-Bobbidi-Boo!" I said firmly.

Nothing happened. Of course, right?

I concentrated. Funny thing about concentration—you don't realize how little you do it until you finally do it. Fact is, I don't think I'd ever *truly* concentrated on anything until that moment with the very big lion in the very small room.

"Turn into *your natural form!*" I wielded the drumstick again. "Do it! DO IT—I'M SERIOUS!"

Boom! Lightning, sparks, acrid smell, et cetera, and lots of smoke.

I waved my hand in front of my face so I could see, and it became clear that there was no more lion. But there was no Byron, Disgrace to Kids Everywhere, either.

Whit and I looked at each other in amazement but also utter confusion.

Then I heard low-volume scuffling and squeaking sounds over by the door.

"Hmm," I said.

"Hmm," said Whit.

I don't know if my saying "natural form" translated into magicspeak the way "pumpkin" had translated into "lion," but clearly this was closer to the mark.

Because Byron "Tattling Weasel" Swain was now an actual *weasel*.

Chapter 46

Whit

"MY SISTER—WOW! Dang, you're good," I told her.

"Yep," she agreed. "I'm a bad, scary witch, all right."

"I'm so glad you didn't discover these powers earlier, like when you were a little kid and I used to tease you about your hair," I said, and she grinned like she'd just won the lottery.

As we peered down, the Little Beastie Formerly Known as Byron reared up on its hind feet and hissed angrily.

"He liked being a lion better," I guessed.

Just then the door to our cell crashed open, and the Matron stood there with two of her nastiest, beefiest armed guards. Call 'em Joe and Schmo. We did.

"What was that awful, terrible noise?" she shouted, raking the room with her eyes.

"Uh...what noise?" I asked with the innocence of a Scout at jamboree.

"It sounded like...a lion roaring," she said, her corpse-white skin turning self-consciously pink.

"*Okay...*," I said, frowning slightly and arching my eyebrows. "A lion? Here? In our cell?"

The two guards looked at each other. Out of the corner of my eye, I saw the weasel slink through the open door, keeping to the shadows.

"Where is Junior Informant Swain?" the Matron demanded.

"I'm sorry, but he left, Matron," I said, forcing myself to sound respectful. "He only stayed a minute. Read us the abridged riot act, though. He's tough."

"You're lying!" Her cavernous nostrils flared wide, making white lines on either side of her formidable nose. The next thing I knew, she lunged forward, jabbing the stun gun against the small of my back.

Chapter 47

Whit

I FROZE—fully expecting to drop with excruciating pain as I had before, maybe pass out—but all I felt was a little . . . tickling sensation.

At first I thought maybe she hadn't charged the stun gun properly, but I looked down and saw the evil blue sparks and smelled the ozone, just like before, yet there was no terrible pain. Nada.

The Matron glared, waiting for me to fall down, so I obligingly groaned and sank to my knees, dragging my hands along the wall as if I didn't have the strength to keep upright. I flashed a quick wink at Wisty so she'd know I was faking.

In the meantime, the guards took their posts just outside the door while the Matron scrutinized the tiny air-shaft window. It was clearly too small for us to have thrown Byron out of, at least in his former shape.

She investigated the bathroom for what seemed like an eternity, like maybe we had flushed him down the john and she'd find his hair gel for evidence.

Then it hit me that the Matron and her lackeys had left the door to the hallway open. I glanced at Wisty and saw she'd noticed too. We started to slink toward it, but we could see the guards' arms outside, holding stun guns at the ready. Was there any way we could take them? Maybe Wisty could turn them into toads?

I saw something dart into the room then. A shadow. It instantly blended with the deep gloom along the far wall. Wisty's eyes widened—she'd seen it too. We exchanged puzzled, worried glances.

The Matron glared at us suspiciously. "I'll be back." Then she stomped out.

As she was passing one of the guards, she had a last-minute idea and tapped her stun gun against his chest. Instantly "Joe" screamed and dropped like a sack of hot potatoes. We all stared at his muscular body, twitching on the ground like a monster eel.

The Matron looked at him, looked at the stun gun, then slammed our door, locking it.

"So," Wisty asked, "stun guns not so effective on you any longer?"

I couldn't help chuckling. "Apparently not," I said, peering into the shadows again. I was sure I had seen something moving. . . .

"Either I've developed some serious tolerance, or our powers are growing—"

I broke off as I saw one shadow separating from another. A person-shaped shadow. It moved toward us.

"Oh my God, Whit," Wisty said. "Now I'm seeing fairies."

Chapter 48

Whit

"NOT EXACTLY," it said in a voice that just about stopped me from breathing.

As the shadow moved closer to the meager light, it became more three-dimensional. Right before our eyes, the shape...filled in, until it—*she*—looked incredibly real. And beautiful.

"Celia," I whispered. "You came."

"Celia!" confirmed Wisty. "You came from *where?*"

She smiled at us both, what little light there was raking across her face. She didn't seem as pale now, and I took that as a good sign. Hopeful.

"Hi, Wisty," said Celia, giving her sweetest smile. She'd always been supernice to Wisty. And everybody else, for that matter—geeks, jocks, Goths, little kids—it made no difference to Celia. She found the best in people—especially me.

"B-but...*how?*" Wisty stammered as Celia moved toward us without a sound. And suddenly I noticed that something else was different—she had no scent. She'd always worn this wild-rose perfume, and every time I smelled it, my heart thudded a little and my blood seemed to pump faster. But now when I breathed deep, all I could smell was the dank Hospital.

"Can I...hold you?" I asked.

"I don't think so, but we can try," Celia said, getting more emotional. "Oh, Whit...please try. I need you to hold me."

"I'd leave you two alone," said Wisty, "but there's nowhere for me to go. Sorry. I'll just...close my eyes."

Very gently I tried to put my arms around Celia. And I could actually feel her again. She definitely wasn't smoke or an illusion, but she wasn't exactly solid either. I tried to push aside her hair, to nuzzle her neck—something that had gotten me to many happy places. But I couldn't move her hair.

Celia understood instantly. She smiled and tossed her hair back. That familiar gesture...I never thought I'd see it again. It was probably my imagination, but it felt like a breeze of fresh air washed through the cell as she did it. Tears welled in my eyes. I couldn't help it.

"*This* is why I love you," she whispered. "You're something else, Whit. I don't understand everything that's happening, but I know more than you do. After I saw you, I couldn't find you right away, and none of the Curves could help me get back here to the Hospital. The Shadowland is a dark, complicated place...very easy to get lost in...for a very long time.

"Then your weasel came racing through one of the portals into the Shadowland. He was the one who showed me how to get here.

"So I've come to bust you out of this wretched Hospital. Before they execute you both. The only problem is, to get out of here we have to travel through the Shadowland. Whit—and Wisty, you can open your eyes now—I'm not sure we'll be able to get back out. You could be there forever."

Chapter 49

Wisty

SO FAR THE ONLY THING that completely made sense to me was the word "weasel." I didn't know what the heck a Curve was, or anything at all about portals or the Shadowland. And I was still too overwhelmed with this bittersweet sadness—seeing Whit and Celia together again, the way they were looking at each other—to process too many more details about our twisted new reality.

Celia was by far my favorite of Whit's girlfriends and admirers. For one thing, she always had time to talk to me. And even listen to me. For another, Celia was everything I wasn't, and secretly wanted to be. I used to stare at myself in the mirror—with my too-fair skin, my too-many freckles, and this awful splotch of red hair—and think that nature, genetics, and karma had really shafted me.

"Um," I said, not even knowing where to begin, "you found our weasel? Didn't you just *hate* it?"

Celia smiled again, looking like a supermodel, and not

the stuck-up or shallow kind. "No, I didn't hate it. It was a live weasel, not a Half-light, like me. So I knew it was important somehow."

"What's a Half-light?" I couldn't help asking.

"I'm a Half-light. Because...well...I'm dead, Wisty."

I shook my head. "Don't say that, Celia. Listen, Whit and I—well, you probably know the deal—we kind of turned out to have, um, *powers*. Maybe we can save you."

"It's not simple like that, Wisty," Celia continued patiently. "Let me explain some more. The Half-lights, or spirits, live in the Shadowland."

I couldn't keep the questions from coming. "The Shadowland? Is that anything like...purgatory? Limbo? Isn't that where dead babies go?"

Celia winced. "Well, um, *no* to dead babies, but *yes* to purgatory and limbo, only the Shadowland is, well, kind of its own dimension of reality. There's more than just the present, the here and now that you're used to. Anyway, Half-lights can sometimes come and go through portals into your world. Portals are holes between the two realms. They develop over time but can disappear just as randomly. While the openings are there, Half-lights and certain people and animals—called Curves—can go through them. Like your weasel did."

"He's not exactly *our* weasel," Whit said. "He's our enemy, actually. A vicious little scumbag."

"Well, he knew you," said Celia. "He told us all about you. He told us you're scheduled to be executed tomorrow."

"I can't believe he just blurted that stuff out," I said. "He's not exactly a cooperative weasel."

Celia rolled her eyes. "He didn't want to tell us anything," she said. "We tortured him. Then he told us."

That sounded interesting. "Tortured?"

Celia nodded. "We held him down and tickled his little weasel belly until tears came out of his eyes. In the end he was begging to tell us everything he knew. I don't think he wants to come back here now."

"I don't blame him," said Whit. "If I could get out of here, I wouldn't come back either. Not in a million years."

"Speaking of which, baby," said Celia to Whit, "it's about time for us to go. We have to risk it . . . the Shadowland."

I nodded, but my mind was somewhere else. If Whit and Celia could be together now, why couldn't they be together forever? Somehow, some way, I wanted to bring Celia back from the dead for Whit.

Could a witch do that?

Chapter 50

Wisty

"WE'VE GOT TO HURRY," said Celia. "I can't stay in your world much longer. We have to get you two out of this godforsaken place."

"Oh, why didn't *we* think of that?" Whit cracked, and Celia just smiled.

I don't know how she does it. Things Whit says that make me almost scream in frustration just make Celia laugh. Did I mention how much I like her?

"As soon as we get the door open," Celia went on, touching Whit's cheek with her hand, "you have to jet out of this cell and run like crazy for the nearest portal to get to the Underworld."

"The Underworld?" Whit asked. *"Celia?"*

"Sorry. I keep forgetting—you're new to all this. The Underworld is everything that isn't the Overworld," Celia said, as if it were as obvious a concept as, say, peanut butter and jelly. "Or at least it was till the New Order started messing with things."

Celia was faced with our two blank stares.

"Sorry. Let me be clearer. The New Order now controls almost all of the Overworld—that's the, uh, regular world that you're used to. The Underworld contains the rest of the known universe—the Shadowland and other dimensions. For the moment, the N.O. doesn't run the show in all those places. But they're trying. The One Who Is The One is after total control.

"Somehow, the two of you are in his way. That's a puzzle *you* have to solve."

"Okay," said Whit, looking determined. "Where's the portal? Is it in the bathroom?"

"No, that one's gone already," Celia said. "It took me a while to find another."

"And so the portal you used is," I prompted, "like, where exactly?"

"End of the hall," Celia said. "Past the dogs, unfortunately. Then you just rush toward the wall and throw yourself into it. You'll go through."

"You're kidding me," Whit said. "C'mon, Celia. Get real."

"No fair," I whined. "Isn't the *definition* of a portal, like, an *opening*? In fact, I'm pretty sure my fourth-grade teacher would've called a brick wall an 'antonym' of the word 'portal.'"

"Wisty, please trust me on this. I know you won't want

to run into a wall at full speed, but it's the only way you'll escape. You've got to do what I tell you."

I looked at Celia, hoping this wasn't an elaborate hoax. Was she really the Celia that Whit and I had known? What if this was a trap?

"We can run through the wall," Whit said, sounding grim but very determined. The old QB was back. "When is all this supposed to happen?"

Celia looked at us. "In about a minute."

Chapter 51

Whit

OKAY, IN TERMS OF emergency preparedness, "in about a minute" never, ever falls under the category "enough time."

What choice did we have, though? It was either run through a wall or get executed.

I looked at Wisty. "Got your drumstick?"

She held it up. "Check. Drumstick."

I picked up my journal, stuffing it into my jumpsuit. "You think you can do anything about the devil dogs?" I asked lightning girl.

Wisty shrugged doubtfully. "I'll try, Whit. But I'm still learning this stuff."

"Okay, here's what we can do," I said. "Once we get out of here, we'll run like mad to that hallway. You'll have a couple of seconds to try something with the dogs. If you can't pull it off, then I'll just tear through like I usually do to get food. I'll hold your hand. You run as fast as you can, even if we get bitten. It's okay to scream but not to stop!"

Wisty swallowed, looking a little freaked but resolute. "Gotcha. Scream. Don't stop."

Celia nodded. "I'll be right there behind you. Of course, I'm biteproof."

I had a really bad thought: "What if the Matron and the horror-show guards throw themselves through the portal too?"

"They won't," said Celia. "Unless they're secretly Curves. If they're Straight and Narrows, they'll just hit the wall. It could be kind of funny, actually."

Oh good. So we had that to look forward to. I added "Straight and Narrows" to the growing list of terms I had to ask Celia about.

I wiped my damp palms on my jumpsuit. We were going to, like, "cross over" to the other side now, right? Wasn't that sort of like *dying*?

Chapter 52

Whit

"QUICK! RAP THREE TIMES on your door. Hard!" Celia urged. "Now! I really can't be here much longer, Whit. My spirit could die."

"What does *that* mean?" I said.

"Just hit that door, Whit—three times!"

I pounded as if my life depended on it—which it did. The next second, we heard the lock go *click*.

I turned to Celia. "What just happened?"

"Whit, *go!*" she said. "The door's unlocked."

Celia grabbed for the knob . . . and kind of went through the door completely.

"I always forget," she muttered. "I can't grab things anymore."

I yanked it open for Celia, took Wisty's hand, and poked my head out into the hallway.

The Matron was away from her desk, talking with

some guards about thirty yards down the hall to the right. So far, at least, they seemed unaware of us. I couldn't see whoever—*whatever*—had unlocked our door. Was it my magic? Celia's? Wisty's?

"Go!" Celia said in my ear, so Wisty and I leaped out of our cell and raced toward the dreaded nurses' station.

We skidded around the corner just as we heard the Matron screaming bloody murder from behind. "Stop them! They're trying to escape! Sound the alarm! Shoot to kill! Take no prisoners!"

Another six or seven strides, and we were at Wolf Row. The floor was literally shaking with guards, and the Matron was thundering after us.

"Hurry, hurry," I told Wisty. "Do your stuff. Make 'em into puppies. Stuffed dogs."

Wisty stood just out of reach of the snarling, barking animals. She held up her drumstick like it was a conductor's baton and the hounds were her orchestra. Nice image, but would it work?

Out of the corner of my eye, I saw the guards and the Matron round the bend.

"Freeze!" commanded Wisty loudly, and waved her stick at the dogs.

For a split second, nothing happened, and I gripped her hand, ready to boogie down the hellway. Then the dogs' yelps and barks strangled to sudden silence.

The animals actually froze in place.

Paws were raised, jaws gaped hungrily—several of the beasts were actually in midlunge at us, standing on their hind legs.

"Yes! *I'm a witch!*" Wisty yelled. "Let's go!"

"Perfect! You're amazing, Wisty!" said Celia, right by my side. "There's the portal!" She pointed near the end of the hallway, at a blank wall that showed no obvious signs of opening up or turning into foam or anything like that. "Run as fast as you can! Now!"

I couldn't get out of my mind those videos we'd watched in driver's-ed class. Crash-test dummies going *kablooey* in slow mo as the cars smashed into walls.

No, I thought. *Think "victory, victory, victory."*

The Matron and the guards were right behind us, halfway through the frozen dogs. So I rushed at the wall like I was a quarterback again—and I went right through the portal to the other side.

But I lost my grip on Wisty's hand. She just slipped away, screaming my name.

I lost Wisty!

Chapter 53

Whit

MY FEET LANDED on something hard, maybe a stone floor, and I somersaulted to a stop.

I leaped up. *"Wisty!"* I yelled. *"Sis?"*

From the Shadowland side of things, I could see her still standing in the Hospital hallway. It was like I was looking through a pane of thick, wavy glass. Celia was trying to grab hold of Wisty, but she couldn't, of course. It's a ghost thing, I guess.

Then I saw Wisty raise her drumstick again and shout, "Release!"

Instantly the mad dogs roared back to life, surging around the guards and the Matron like a gigantic pileup in the middle of a ball field. Not only were the dogs released from their spell but they were released from their chains. One guard made it through the animals and rushed toward Wisty, starting to level his stun gun.

A dog broke free from the pack and bounded after him, baying like a hound released from hell.

The guard and the crazed dog were right on Wisty's and Celia's heels as they rushed toward the...well, whatever it was.

"Watch out!" I screamed. *"Right behind you!"*

Wisty closed her eyes and pitched herself through the portal, stumbling right into me. "Whit!" she screamed. "It actually worked!"

Celia was with her, and right behind Celia, the dog dived paws-first through the portal. It came at us in midair, hit the floor, and skidded to a stop. Suddenly it looked not so much fierce and deranged as totally confused.

We all glanced back just as the guard slammed into the wall face-first. Behind him, the Matron's white-uniformed figure was still being attacked by the pack of ferocious animals. Her enormous arms flailed, her stun gun knocked from her hand, spinning away. Then she disappeared under the pile of snapping mouths. *Bye-bye.*

"There's someone who's working out some serious karma," said Wisty, but instead of relishing the sight, I reached out to try to hug Celia in a moment of relief that we'd made it through to the other side.

It didn't matter how awkward and ridiculous it was, trying to hug a ghost. That's the cool thing about love. In my opinion anyway.

Just then a whimper made me jerk my head around.

"*The dog*," said Wisty, staring at it, expecting the worst.

"No, it must be okay—it's a Curve dog," Celia marveled. "A Curve is anyone who has access to the Underworld, whether they know it or not. This dog didn't know it. It must not have been fully brainwashed by the Straight and Narrows."

Its lips curled up in an ingratiating grin as if to say, "*Sorry I tried to eat you.*" Then the dog lowered its head further and sort of slunk toward us, low to the ground.

"It looks deeply sorry," Celia said. "I wish I could pet it. Go ahead, Wisty. Pet it."

"Maybe some other time," Wisty said reluctantly. "We have a lot of history to work out first." But then the dog sat and gazed up at her longingly, with the saddest brown eyes, looking much less horrible and insane than it had in Hell's Kennel.

Wisty looked at me, and I knew what she was going to ask.

"You're crazy," I said, sighing.

"I'm nothing if not forgiving," she said earnestly.

"Well, okay," I grumbled. "Maybe it'll be a watchdog or something useful in the Shadowland."

Wisty winked at me, then looked at the dog and patted one knee. The animal stood up cautiously.

"You can come," she told it, then added, "It's a she. I'm going to call her Feffer."

"Okay. Feffer it is," I conceded. "Now let's go meet some Curves and Half-lights and locate some new portals."

Then there was a terrible crash—and we looked and saw the Matron's face smashed up against the wall to the portal.

"Not a Curve," said Wisty with a broad smile. "Didn't think so."

BOOK THREE

BRAVE NEW WORLDS

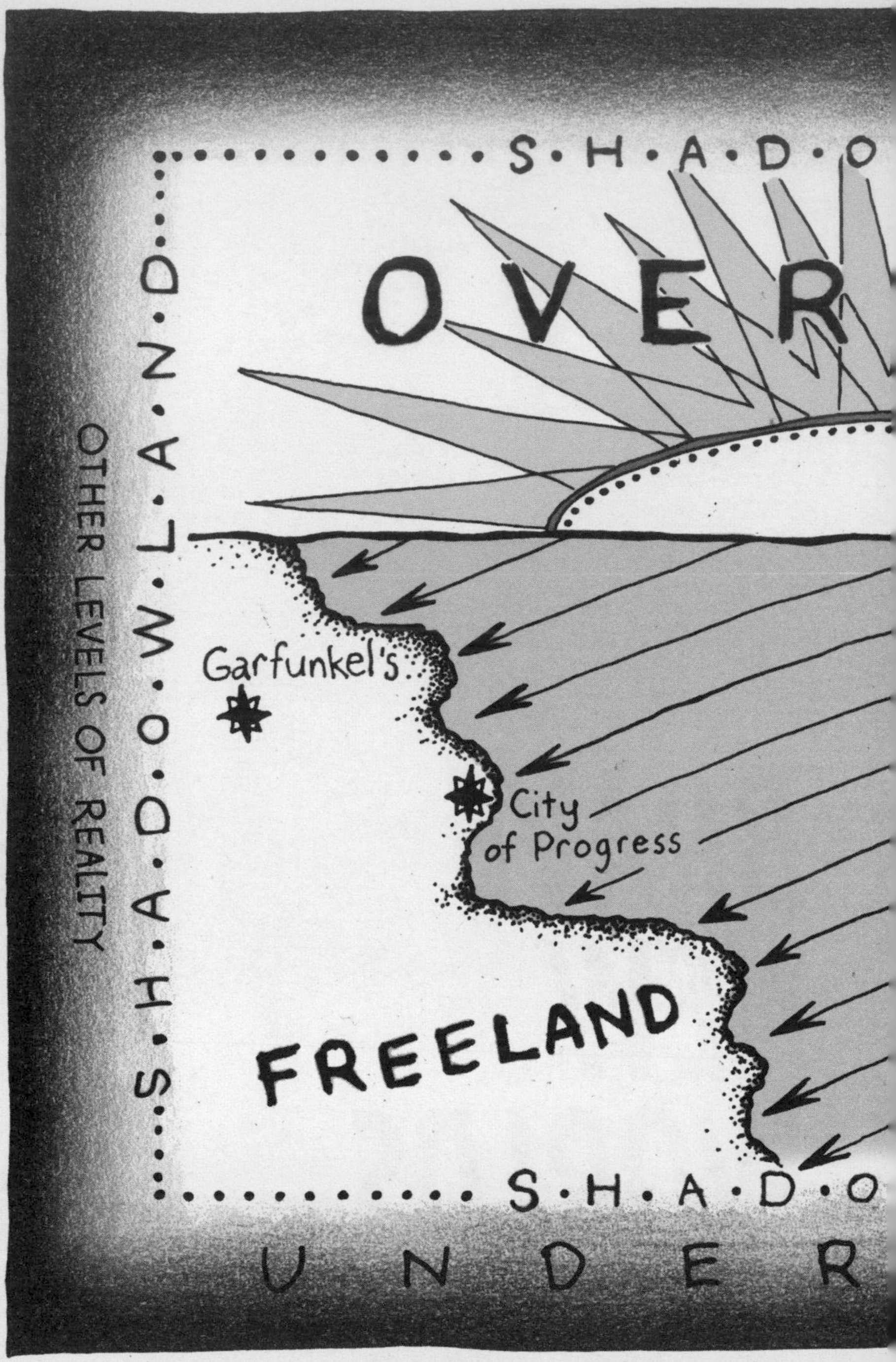
S·H·A·D·O
OVER
Garfunkel's
City of Progress
FREELAND
S·H·A·D·O·W·L·A·N·D
OTHER LEVELS OF REALITY
S·H·A·D·O
UNDER

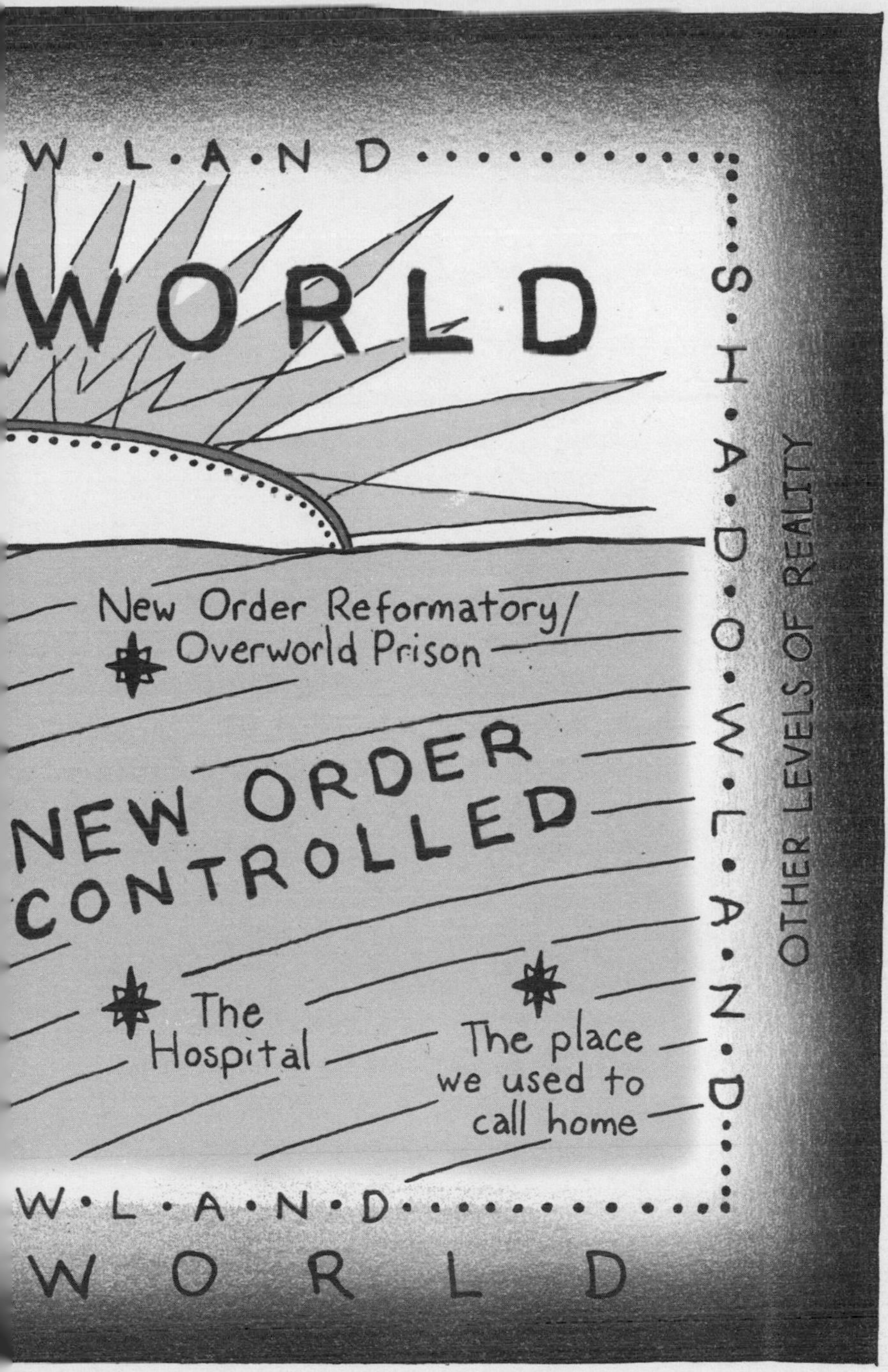
W·L·A·N·D
WORLD
New Order Reformatory/
Overworld Prison
NEW ORDER
CONTROLLED
The
Hospital
The place
we used to
call home
S·H·A·D·O·W·L·A·N·D
OTHER LEVELS OF REALITY
W·L·A·N·D
W O R L D

Chapter 54

Wisty

WHIT GRABBED ME in a bear hug that felt extraordinarily reassuring. "We're outta there! We're safe from her now."

Safe from the Matron, maybe. But in the grand scheme of things, I wasn't so sure we hadn't just leaped out of the frying pan and into someplace a lot worse.

As I tried to get my bearings, it became apparent that this "other side" wasn't at all what I had expected. For one thing, it was cold. Not freezing cold, but a sort of damp, penetrating cold that hurt your lungs. For another, *there wasn't anything there*.

"Um...Celia...where are we again?" I asked.

"This is the Shadowland."

I looked around. It wasn't quite right to call the Shadowland a "land" at all. There were no trees, grass, buildings, water, sun—or, for that matter, anything but fog and haze.

"This is your...home?" I whispered, hugging myself for warmth and turning completely around. The portal, which I thought had just been at my back, was gone now.

"I would never call the Shadowland home," Celia said with a head shake. "And I hope neither of you do either."

I couldn't see...*anything*, really, beyond Whit, Celia, and Feffer. It was like we were standing in a room with a gray backdrop, and everything beyond about ten or fifteen feet in any direction seemed to fade into hazy nothingness. It was unnerving, not having anything to focus my eyes on. A wave of claustrophobic panic washed over me.

"Celia..." Whit looked around uneasily. "We have to get you out of this place. You got us out of the Hospital. We can—"

"Whit, let it go," Celia interrupted gently. "You may be a wizard, but no one can bring dead people back to life. Not even The One Who Is The One. Remember that. It's a fact of life and death. It's how you get past grief."

Feffer started trotting off to explore, or maybe to find a Half-light squirrel to chase. The dog seemed to be the only one of us that had a sense of direction here, so I followed her lead. "What's out here, Feffer?"

"Wisty, *no!*" Celia shouted.

I almost got mad at being yelled at like a two-year-old wandering away from Mommy at the mall—but I knew Celia wasn't exactly the nervous type. And she sounded seriously freaked.

"This can be a very dangerous place for humans. Your senses don't work here like they do in your world...and if you get any farther away from me and Whit, we could be entirely lost to one another. Especially because it's possible to take a path that will lead you into a subdimension completely different from ours."

I didn't understand the dimension part, but I whirled around in a panic nonetheless.

I couldn't see Feffer anymore.

"Feffer! Here, girl!" I whistled. "Come back, girl!" Strangely, I already felt an attachment to the reformed hellhound.

Feffer came trotting right back to me, and I knelt down to hug her. The warm scent of her fur seemed very real and comforting in this hollow place.

"Well, Feffer apparently didn't have a problem," I said, puzzled, as the dog, sniffing the ground, wandered off again.

"I said, dangerous for *humans*," Celia clarified. "Feffer's an animal, and she has animal instincts. We don't use sight to get around in here. Half-lights and others who are tuned in to extrasensory forces have a much easier time navigating the Shadowland. Humans who've found the portals have usually gotten lost here. *Forever.*"

As if to punctuate the horror of this thought, we heard a distant moaning sound. Whit involuntarily grabbed my hand.

"Lost Ones," said Celia. "They're not close yet, and that's the way we want to keep it. Believe me."

"What would they do to us?" I asked.

"They'd..." Calm-and-collected Celia looked as if she might lose it. "Forget it, Wisty. It's way too grim to talk about right now. Let's just get you somewhere safe."

Chapter 55

Wisty

"CELIA! YOU'RE ALL RIGHT!" we heard someone call out, and a tall blond girl, maybe Whit's age, came bounding into view. She was a Half-light, I assumed, even though I'd never pictured dead girls wearing tank tops and pleated skirts...and chewing bubble gum. *And do dead girls really need glasses?* Maybe it was a fashion statement.

"You got your friends out!" the girl said, then hugged Celia, the way Half-lights hug. Hard to describe.

"This is Susan," said Celia. "Susan, this is Whit Allgood and his sister, Wisty. Remember me telling you about Whit?"

Susan rolled her eyes. "Yes. Mr. Wonderful. Mr. Sensitive. Mr. Washboard Tummy. I think you mentioned Whit once or twice. Total pukka kind of guy. You said he was a work of art."

I blinked. "Pukka" sounded a little pukey to me. Celia wasn't the least embarrassed, though Whit got a tad pink in the cheeks.

"Welcome," said Susan, who seemed funny and nice. "Glad you got out of the Hospital. That place is a total mingus. It's where I was executed. For chewing gum on the street. I think."

"I have to get these two to Freeland before any Lost Ones spot them," said Celia.

"I agree," said Susan. "I saw a small pack of them only a few minutes from here. They've probably sensed there are living humans around."

"Well, let's reunite these guys with their erlenmeyer weasel and get them out of here."

Susan and Celia had started to lose me with all of their weird lingo until Celia mentioned Byron Traitor Suck-up. I'd forgotten all about him.

"He's not exactly *our* weasel," repeated Whit.

Just then we heard another distant chorus of spine-chilling moans.

"We don't need to wait for him, *really*," I said, cold sweat breaking out all over me.

"It's no bother," said Susan. "And we have to meet somebody else here anyway. In fact, here he comes. Yo, Sasha!" she yelled as a boy came running into view. I was starting to get used to *partially* solid people, so his opaqueness seemed out of place in the Shadowland. Then I realized he was probably a regular kid like us.

"You're safe, Celia," Sasha said with relief as she introduced us. He seemed older than me but maybe younger than Whit, and he had longish black hair and dark-blue eyes. He wore a Navy SEALS ball cap on backward, and his T-shirt read FREEDOM *SHOULD* BE FREE. I also noticed he was carrying a spool that trailed string into the gray haze behind him.

"So you find your way around here using *string?*" I asked him.

"Yeah," he said. "I have some portal-sensing abilities, but it's best to have backup. And bread crumbs are useless. But let's talk about all that later. I heard a pack of Lost Ones on my way over here." He was serious but wore an expression of easy confidence—which, in a split second, disappeared.

"Look out!" he yelled, and leaped in front of us to block the shape emerging from the fog. But it was just Feffer.

"Oh," he said, embarrassed. "I'm guessing you brought a dog."

"This is Feffer," I said. "She came through the portal with us."

"Cool, a Curve dog," said Sasha, getting down on his knees to pet her. "You sure it's gonna like your weasel?"

"He's not *our* weasel," Whit repeated. "Actually, that little rodent, that *varmint,* wanted to execute us."

Just then another moan—sounding closer this time—cut through the gloaming. Celia's beautiful eyes became a little sad. "Sasha, you need to lead them to the Freeland portal *right now.*"

Whit turned to her. "Can't you come with us? You have to."

Celia nodded. "Of course I will. But I can't stay long,

Whit. Or I'll...cease to be. That's another fact of life and death."

"Let's get out of here!" said a voice at my feet. I looked down and almost screamed.

"You're taking the weasel," Susan said firmly. "Incidentally, he needs a bath. And to be taught some manners. And some social skills."

I glared down at him. "No. You can't come. I hate your guts."

He sat up on his haunches, beady black eyes boring into mine. "You did this to me."

Sasha looked impressed. "You taught a weasel to speak?!"

"I was human," said Byron. "And *she* is a witch."

Sasha looked even more impressed.

"And don't you forget it," I said proudly. "Feffer? Meet Byron Traitor Suck-up. You may eat him."

Chapter 56

Wisty

BUT FEFFER DIDN'T HAVE A CHANCE to find out what weasel tasted like. Because just then we all spotted the first thing other than ourselves that we'd ever seen in the Shadowland, and it was, in fact, a bunch of shadows.

They were distant and flickered out of sight as soon as we looked directly at them, but there was no question we didn't want to get any closer.

Celia, Susan, and Sasha immediately put their fingers to their mouths, telling us to be quiet, and then—as Susan and Celia just kind of faded into the gray—Sasha did that little commando gesture indicating we should follow him.

With the weasel clinging to my pants leg and shaking like one of those toys that vibrate when you pull their tails, we fell into line behind him and jogged along his string toward what I prayed would be our escape.

"Sasha," I panted after we'd been running for a minute or so, "did it just get really cold in here or what?"

"It's the Lost Ones. Among other things, they absorb the heat of the living."

"So," I said, an uncomfortable realization dawning on me, "does that mean...they're close?"

"No more talking" was all he said.

But then he stopped. He was holding the end of the string. And there was no portal there.

"Something broke the string," he said, fear flickering in his brilliant eyes.

From behind us, a chorus of moans added an ugly exclamation point to his statement.

Then Sasha shook his head like a swimmer trying to get water out of his ears and took off into the fog.

Byron, scared past coherent speech, chattered nonsense as we followed. I felt the cold on my back getting more and more intense.

And then I did something incredibly stupid: I looked back over my shoulder.

Twenty or more shadows—crooked, tall, short, bent, hobbling, but all supernaturally fast—were chasing after us. Just yards behind us now.

They were indistinct, flickering, inconstant, but one of them loomed up and, with the most horrible, ravenous, yellow eyes, seemed to *see* me.

And then I did something even more stupid: I stopped and screamed.

Whit immediately scooped me up and raced after Sasha. I couldn't stop myself from yelling, and the boys seemed to know it. They didn't even try to shush me. I guess they knew the game was up—either Sasha would guide us to the portal in time or he wouldn't.

And then we'd find out exactly what it was the Lost Ones did to people.

Chapter 57

Wisty

"OKAY," SASHA SAID, stopping suddenly. "Brace yourselves."

My heart leaped. Bracing, I could handle. Getting mauled by soul-eating shadow creatures, not so much.

But where was the portal? All I saw was more fog. Was the portal here? Where?

Just then Feffer—who was, sweet dog, running tail guard several yards behind us—whimpered piteously.

"Feffer!" I stopped my own whimpering and yelled as the dog, unable to control herself, raced past toward a patch of fog that, I suddenly noticed, seemed to be rotating like a sideways whirlpool. She was bleeding. Badly. It looked as if something had gashed her left side with a garden rake. And the fright in her eyes—she looked more like a terri-fied puppy than a former New Order hellhound.

But before I could even think to reach out to comfort her, she was past me and leaping into the swirling vapor. And she was gone.

"That's our portal," said Sasha. "You two next. And be careful," he said. "Freeland can be pretty wild."

Wild, I could also handle—I'd have happily signed up for a deep-jungle camping trip with a pack of hungry jaguars. Anything but this nightmare scene. But I couldn't joke about it to Sasha. For one thing, my teeth were chattering too hard to talk.

We were suddenly confronted with a cold so intense it burned—and it was coming from *in front* of us.

One of the Lost Ones had somehow gotten in between us and the portal.

Maybe if pain, hatred, and suffering were mixed in equal parts, somehow given shape, and dipped in black paint, you'd come close to what we saw now. Although there was something disturbingly, hauntingly human about its shadow-filled face. There was no skin, just sort of a flickering, shadowy surface where you would expect to see a forehead, cheeks, nose . . . and then there were the eyes. No pupils. Just slits, yellow-orange, flickering like torches you'd see on the walls of hell.

I wanted nothing more than to scream, but I was now officially paralyzed by the frozen air and my terror.

I squinted my eyes against the cold and watched helplessly as other Lost Ones moved in around us. We were surrounded.

Then—and I don't know where he got the strength or courage—Sasha stepped toward the one directly in front of the portal, ignoring its clicking finger-claws and looking into its deathly yellow eyes.

"You got us," he said. "But you'll want me to explain this to you." He reached into his pants pocket and pulled out a piece of paper. "It's a map. With it, I can show you where to find a portal—not like this one, which won't work for your kind—that can take you out of the Shadowland. A way back home."

Somehow the horrible creature seemed to understand and appreciate what Sasha was saying.

And then, with a masterful flourish, Sasha crumpled the paper and threw it to the ground, causing the creature to leap after it with an earsplitting shriek of anger.

And then Sasha fairly tackled Whit and me into the portal, and the three of us plunged through, Byron Hateful Suck-up Weasel clinging to my pants leg with all four paws, the insufferable little creep.

There was an electric, tingly feeling that got stronger and stronger until my body began to shake like I was being tossed around in the back of a horse-drawn cart barreling down a cobblestone road at fifty miles an hour.

And then, suddenly, we were through—and *outside*, it seemed. The initial sensation was of wind—and it felt amazing, as if it were the first fresh air that had touched my skin in years.

I got my balance, then stopped in shock and looked around. "Oh. My. God."

Chapter 58

Wisty

WE STOOD ON A DRY, rubble-covered hillside. There wasn't much to it, but the sun was up and the sky was blue. After those horrifying minutes in the Shadowland, I was quite simply shocked by how beautiful the real world was.

"Those Lost-One things are looking to get out of the Shadowland, huh?" Whit asked Sasha as we dusted ourselves off.

"Yeah, they say that's why they cling on to humans so hard. They want us to help them find a way out. And when that doesn't work—which it never does—they settle for stealing your warmth and eating your flesh."

"But you gave them the map. Does that mean they can now find their own way into the real world?" asked Whit.

"Well, (A) I don't think they can read, (B) I'm not sure they could survive in the real world—I sure hope not—and (C) it wasn't a map, it was just a list of things I had to do once I got back to base."

"So you just made all that up on the spot, and fooled those things so we could escape?"

He shrugged and was going to say something, but just then there was a high-pitched whine in the air.

"Incoming!" yelled Sasha, and slammed into me, knocking me down. I hit the ground hard, the air whooshing out of me.

I gasped like a fish on land as a piercing, whistling sound filled my ears, impossibly loud.

Then, *boom!* Make that *BOOM!* I squeezed my eyes shut as the ground shook like an earthquake. Sasha tightened his hold on me, covering my head with his hands. I kind of liked him already.

BOOM! More earthshaking explosions, more trembling, more dust and mud and rubble raining down on our heads.

"Wisty!" Whit yelled.

I wheezed and gasped. "Whit! Feffer!" I choked out. I couldn't see very much because of the smoke and dust everywhere.

It felt like ages, but the trembling finally calmed, and Sasha's weight slowly moved off me. A minute later, it was over. Whatever it was.

"Whew!" Sasha said, grinning. His face was covered with thick dust, except for his mouth and eyes. He reminded me of a freaky circus clown. I guessed I probably looked the same. "Sorry," he told me cheerfully. "Didn't mean to squish you like that."

"It's okay," I said. "I've been squished by worse."

I struggled to sit up, feeling Byron Hateful Suck-up coiled around my neck like a traitorous mink stole. Blinking grit out of my eyes, coughing, shaking off the dust, I looked around.

"What just happened?" I asked, finally seeing Whit. And then Feffer. And Celia.

"Bomb," Sasha said, standing up and slapping off the dirt. "Everyone okay? I guess we must have stepped out into a war zone. Easy to do." It sounded like this was about as ordinary as making a wrong turn en route to the nearest doughnut shop.

Looking around, I saw half-destroyed buildings on what once must have been a normal city block. Craters in the street were big enough to hold trucks. Rubble and dust were everywhere. Twisted metal, broken glass, electric wires, and chunks of cement made a dangerous carpet under our feet.

"Who's bombing us?" I asked, trembling all over. So was Byron—the varmint was now riding on my shoulder, clinging to my hair. "Get *off*," I told him.

"The New Order does bombings every day," Sasha explained. "They know some of us kids are squatting here, so they run air strikes. Then they come looking for us." He shook the hair out of his eyes. "Keeps you on your toes, right?"

"Yeah, nothing like a little shock and awe," Whit said in disbelief.

Sasha turned serious. "We've gotta get you to safety right away, guys."

"Wait," I said. "Whit and I need to look for our parents. We'll go it alone. I mean, we're thankful and everything."

Celia's and Sasha's eyes met and, for once, Sasha's face wasn't so sunny and open. "Um," he said, "we should talk about that, Red."

I glared at Sasha, and my brother spoke up. "Not a nickname she likes. Just FYI."

"The thing is," said Sasha slowly, "it's not safe, or very smart, for you to go off on your own." He took off his ball cap and twisted it in his hands. His thick, jet-black hair fell forward over his eyes. "Sorry about that, Freckles."

Chapter 59

Wisty

"NOT FRECKLES EITHER," suggested Whit. "Or Carrottop."

"Okay," I said. "We have to find my mother and father. *That's* our mission," I stated very clearly. "Family first."

Celia stepped closer to me and put out her hand. I felt a wispy breeze touch my hair and saw the sympathy in her eyes. "Wisty, just listen. Please."

Sasha sighed, then gestured at everything around us. "Look at this screwed-up place. This is what most of the city looks like. The N.O. is taking over 'worthy' communities and shaping everything in its image. The rest, they're just...razing. Like, totaling out of existence."

"Yeah, I'm all sad about that too. It's awful. I get it. But what's that got to do with our mom and dad?"

"Read my lips, friend: things are *bad* all over," he continued. "I don't have any idea where your 'rents might be held, or if they're even...alive." The last word was a whisper.

I stared at him, feeling the blood drain from my face.

"Celia, you saved us. If you could get us out of prison, why can't you help us find our parents? They're alive. I'm sure of it."

Whit stared at Celia, clearly agreeing that I was onto something. A pained expression came over her face, but she didn't respond to what I'd said.

"Look," said Sasha, glancing awkwardly at Celia. I couldn't read his meaning. "Let's just get to safety. We can figure out your next steps when we're in Freeland."

I'd had enough of the sympathy game. Folding my arms across my chest, I stomped my foot like that two-year-old in the shopping mall. "I am not moving one inch until someone gives me a satisfactory answer."

"Wisty," Celia hissed with urgency, "it's really dangerous here. There's stuff worse than bombs, if you can imagine something more terrible than being blown up. We don't know where your parents are yet. And you can't save them anyway . . . *if you're dead.*"

Chapter 60

Whit

"STOP RIGHT WHERE YOU ARE, kids. Let me see some ID. *Now!*"

There were about a dozen of them—make that eleven—all males, probably late teens to midtwenties, big boys with big muscles.

I stepped forward. "Mind if I ask who *you* are, before we show you anything? This is a dangerous part of town, y'know."

The spokesman for the muscled boys looked to be in his early twenties. He was standing on the balls of his feet, ready to start some trouble, I figured.

"You should know who we are. New Order. The Citizen Patrol. We're looking for Strays and Wanteds. Need IDs from all of you. It's the law, friend."

Wisty had moved up alongside me. "Maybe we'd like to see *your* IDs," she said. "Friend."

Meanwhile, a crowd of maybe fifty or sixty "citizens" was forming. Not good.

"Let me take care of this," I said. "Okay?"

Wisty shrugged. "Sure."

"Why don't we all just walk away and *stay* friends?" I said to the group leader. I was hoping to continue talking, but he already had a metal baton out. The crowd was still growing, and getting noisy.

"Citizen Patrol, my butt. More like the Aspiring Dictators' After-School Club," said Wisty, ever the diplomat. "Look at you overgrown goons. Pathetic."

Well, that put them over the top, and they attacked—all eleven of them, batons flailing, the crowd of neighborhood creeps cheering them on.

"My turn." I held Wisty off. "I can do this."

"I can see that," she said. "*Wow*, Whitford."

What she was seeing was that the Citizen Patrol seemed to be moving in slow motion. But actually they weren't. I was just moving very, very fast. I'd felt that I could do this, and I was right.

The lead guy's baton was cocked back, and I snatched it right out of his hand, then kicked his legs out from under him and hit him with a roundhouse punch as he was falling to the sidewalk.

I was moving so fast that I was a blur. I took away all their batons and threw the sticks into a sewer, then knocked them down one by one—except for a beautiful girl. Finally the gang members were sprawled on the ground, groaning and moaning.

"Now, let's see those IDs!" I stood over them and roared, but Sasha was already pulling me away, hurrying all of us up the street and around the nearest corner.

"That was very cool," he said.

"I needed the practice. And I think maybe I could actually get into this wizard thing."

Meanwhile, Celia was on my arm, light as could be. "That was incredible, Whit. Loved it!"

"You definitely show potential," Wisty said, and grinned.

And for that instant, that second, it was like everything was back to the way it was supposed to be, the kind of life I always thought I would have.

But just for that moment.

Chapter 61

Wisty

AFTER WHIT'S DEMONSTRATION of his latest skill set, Sasha led us down a mostly deserted street toward a building with a facade pockmarked by bullet holes and missile strikes. I couldn't believe what I was seeing. Had all this happened while we were at the Hospital? Time felt so... distorted.

"Man, I was hoping I'd been gone long enough for this to stop. All the bombing." Sasha shook his head.

"What do you mean?" I asked.

Sasha shrugged. "I was in the Shadowland for a couple of hours."

Whit frowned. "Why would that be long enough for the, um, New Order to come to their senses and stop bombing?"

Sasha looked at me and Whit in surprise. "You don't know? Celia...?"

"I didn't get the chance to explain everything," Celia said. "We were busy escaping, you know?"

"What don't we know?" I asked. "What else?"

"Lots. For one thing, time is different in the Shadowland," Sasha said, continuing to walk very fast. "In this case, it looks to me like I was probably gone about a month or so. It's not always consistent. Depends on the portal you have to use. Once, I came back and it was earlier that same morning."

Whit and I stared at each other. We had no way of knowing how much time had passed since we'd been captured. We had so many questions.

Apparently the Weasel did too. "So can we step back in time to a day when Wisty actually takes a bath? Her hair is practically turning to dreadlocks."

"Get off me, you ingrate," I said, peeling him away from my neck and plopping him on Feffer's back instead. "Feffer, you're a kinder soul than me. Meet your new best friend."

Feffer barked good-naturedly and wagged her tail. Could she have *ever* been a hellhound?

Then Sasha stopped and pointed.

"Here we go! Home sweet rubble-strewn home! This is where a bunch of us are hanging. Kind of a mingus, but we've fixed it up pretty good."

I looked up and read the broken fluorescent sign, dangling from some wires, for the most amazing luxury department store in the whole world. I'd never been able to afford to even walk through these doors.

"Garfunkel's?" I said breathlessly. "We're gonna live *here*?"

For a moment, I felt like a queen.

Chapter 62

Whit

IN SPITE OF THE DEPRESSING UNCERTAINTY about our parents' whereabouts, Wisty's voice was full of excitement as she said the name of the familiar department store.

"I guess this is, like, your dream come true, huh?" I said to her.

She gave me an ironic smile as Sasha led us through the revolving doors, one of which had been shattered by a rocket, or maybe a runaway tank.

"Totally," Wisty said. "On the one hand, we've been dragged away from our parents, imprisoned, starved, stungunned, denied all basic human rights and freedoms, yada yada yada. On the other hand, look! To my right! It's, like, bra wonderland!"

I was about to make a joke about how it would be a wonder if she even needed one, but she raised her drumstick at me and I shut right up.

"No electricity in here," Sasha said as we walked up a

motionless escalator. "But do you have any idea how flammable perfume is? One of our guys rigged up a little combustion generator. Now we can run a laptop for two hours off a purse-size bottle."

Then something hit me like a cheap shot to the jaw. Did none of these kids have any parents? We were just arriving at the main floor. I started to look around and think, *Every single one of these kids, Half-light or not, has a story ... maybe even a story worse than ours.*

"So how many live here?"

"I guess around two hundred fifty," Sasha mused, "not counting Half-lights, who drift in and out. They can't stay very long, or—"

"We don't need to go into that," said Celia, looking anxious, so very different from the laid-back Celia I'd known before. All I wanted to do was hold her close, tell her everything would be all right. But I wouldn't be able to really hold Celia ever again, would I? And I definitely couldn't tell her that things would be all right.

"We've got our own little pukka society here," said Sasha. "Including, *ta da,* this week's leader!" He'd led us down a corridor to a small bank of offices.

There, sitting at a desk with a little brass-colored MANAGER sign on it, was a cute girl of no more than fifteen; she was busily punching keys on a laptop.

A thick cable ran from the back of the computer to what looked like a small metal garbage can about twenty feet away. I could smell smoke and something like burned lemons coming from the fragrance-fueled laptop. Ugh. I'd never look at perfume the same way again.

The cute girl looked up, brushing long, brown curls over her shoulder. She had a no-nonsense look on her face, no makeup, and was wearing denim overalls over a stained T-shirt.

"Sasha," she said, "it's been, what, forty-three days? We needed you *here*."

"I'm not ducking responsibility, but Celia ran the operation," Sasha said. "And, I should point out, it was a hugely successful one. But there's no accounting for those portals into the Shadowland. Not to mention that we had a prison break to engineer.

"Whit and Wisty"—he turned to us—"meet my former basic-combat partner and this week's leader—you can tell because she's in the manager's office, wearing a MANAGER lapel pin—Janine!"

"Hi," said Janine, not smiling. Still sitting, she reached out and shook my hand like I'd just arrived for a job interview. "Welcome," she said, and then targeted Celia. "Did you get any other kids out of the Hospital?"

Celia shook her head. "There was only one other on the floor, and he wasn't . . . rescuable."

Janine nodded. "Such a shame to find Straight and Narrows afflicting a child. Well, the fight goes on!"

"The fight goes on," Celia echoed, then she turned to me. "I have to go, Whit," she said. "But I'll try to come back."

The word "try" rang in my ears like a funeral bell.

Chapter 63

Whit

HAVE YOU EVER LOST anyone close to you? Then you can imagine my feelings. I loved Celia like crazy. To have her ripped out of my life, over and over again, was unbearable.

I motioned for Celia to come behind one of those mirrored department-store columns for some privacy.

I tried to hold her hands, grasping the shape of them in mine. "Please come back," I told her, looking into her eyes. "I can't stand to lose you again."

She nodded and gave me one of her smiles. "I want to, Whit. I'm so glad...I'm so glad you're alive. Out of everything I miss, I've missed you the most. Oh God, I've missed you."

Then Celia did the most amazing thing.

She came very close to me. Then even closer, until I couldn't see her anymore. I could only feel her, in a way that was more intense and intimate than ever before.

Then we merged. Really—we were like one person.

It was warmth, it was peace, it was pure beauty. I was part of Celia; she was part of me. It was only for a moment, but it seemed as if the feeling were big and powerful enough to last a lifetime. I knew I'd never forget this. Who could?

Finally Celia separated from me. She blew a kiss and ran to a nearby portal, apparently in the boys' shoe department, where she disappeared.

Honestly, it was like I'd just lost half of myself. I lingered by the sneakers and high-tops and wiped tears away. I didn't think I could tell the others what had just happened, not even Wisty.

I couldn't begin to describe being one with Celia . . . and then watching her go away again.

Chapter 64

Wisty

"WHAT DO PEOPLE MEAN by '*this week's* leader'?" I asked Janine. It was one of many questions I would be asking in the next few days. Right now, while Whit was talking—or whatever—with Celia, I was trying to find out more about life at Garfunkel's.

"The grown-ups have amply demonstrated that power corrupts," Janine said, sounding like somebody who was running for office but was actually worthy of the job. "But you do need one person in charge, a final decision-maker, or else everything gets crazy. So we have a leader, but it changes every week. This is my week."

Sasha explained, "The incoming leader spends a day learning the ropes from the previous leader." He leaned against Janine's desk. "And then during the last day they'll train the next person. It works pretty well, actually. The week of September twenty-second was *incredible*."

Janine rolled her eyes.

"You were the leader," I said to Sasha. "I got it."

He grinned. "It was a glorious time for the revolution. My decree about voluntary toilet flushing is still talked about in intellectual circles."

Janine looked at him for a second, then turned to me. "We're very lucky you and Whit are here with us," she said. "We're in need of your skills."

"Skills? Like changing creeps into weasels?" I said.

"In a sense, yes," Janine said matter-of-factly. "It sounds like you're much stronger than the other witches and wizards we've discovered."

"You've got *others?*" I asked, stunned.

"Sort of. But it sounds to me like you're in a totally different category. Not garden-variety cantrip stuff. Of course," she said, ignoring my puzzled look, "I guess we'll see for sure during tomorrow night's raid. We're breaking a bunch of kids out of the Overworld Prison."

I shook my head. "Sorry, Janine. We already told Sasha. We're going to look for our parents."

Janine suddenly grabbed my arm. "You have to help us, Wisty. This is the New Order Reformatory, the same place you were taken after you were kidnapped. In Freeland, we call it the Overworld Prison because it's an evil place. You know that kids' lives depend on it, don't you?"

"Look, I've been there. I know how bad it is. But you have to understand what comes first for us. We've got to find our parents. Period."

Janine was still holding my arm. "You say you do, but you don't know how bad Overworld really is. You have no idea." She looked over at Sasha. "Take them to see Michael Clancy."

Chapter 65

Wisty

WHIT HAD COME BACK from seeing Celia off, and he didn't look too good. No, actually, he looked terrible—for him anyway. Frazzled and scuffed up.

"Who's Michael Clancy?" he wanted to know.

"No idea. Somebody they want us to see about a prison break." I raised my voice for Sasha to hear. He was leading the way. "Who's Michael Clancy?" I called.

"He's right in here," Sasha said, and opened the door to a small, dark room. There was a single mattress on the floor.

"I'm Michael," a soft voice said. "What do you want with me?"

"Tell them your story," said Sasha. He turned to us. "Sit down with Michael, and listen. You can sit there on his mattress. There's plenty of room."

There was room, because Michael was one of the skinniest kids I'd ever met. He reminded me of pictures of famine victims and people in refugee camps I'd seen...and that brought back images of Overworld Prison and the time we'd spent there.

"Hello, Michael," I said.

"Hey, Mike," said Whit.

Not only was the boy nearly wasted away but his eyes looked dead to me. Still, there was something intense about him.

He never asked our names, just went right into his story.

"Memory is a liar, you know that, don't you?" he began. "But I'm sure what I'm going to tell you captures the truth anyway, even if all the details are wrong, which I don't think they are. But maybe so."

"Sure, Michael," I said, just to let him know we were listening closely. He sounded so much older than he looked. I was almost afraid to hear what had happened to him.

"The soldiers, all in black, their boots spit-shined, came for us that morning at the prison, and I believe the sun was already up. There were forty or more of us in this particular cell block. Ages, I'd say, between five and sixteen. Males and females. Many different hues, in terms of skin color, I mean. All 'Extremely Dangerous.'

"They took us, marched us downstairs to a courtyard. There were only a couple of guards in the yard, so I don't think they expected trouble from us. They didn't get much, as we were too tired, too hungry — already broken, for the most part.

"There was this unbelievable wind, very much like a

twister, and then this tall, bald man was right there in front of us. He smelled of almonds, I think.

"He never said a word, never identified himself, though I believe he may have been The One Who Is The One. He looked at us with such disdain, you know, like we were so far beneath him. Then he just...flicked his wrist. Just that. *Flick.*

"There was nothing left of us, except for smoke...and the smell of skin burning. He had...I don't know...*vaporized* everyone. Then he was gone. And I was still there, like I am now. Don't ask, don't you dare ask. I have no idea why I was spared. I don't even care anymore."

Michael Clancy looked at Sasha. "There, I've told my story. Now please take them away."

Chapter 66

Wisty

IT TOOK ME SEVERAL HOURS just to begin to get over Michael Clancy, to wrap my mind around what he had said.

Have you ever felt like your head was taking in so much new and tragic and complicated information that it was about to blow right off your shoulders? Take that feeling, and then eat something really disgusting that makes you want to throw up for hours, and you'll be right about where I was at the moment.

Let's review:

1. I, everyday ordinary Wisty, am a witch. Washboard-tummy Whit is a wizard. We don't exactly know how to control our powers.
2. Whit and I were sentenced to death by an insidious individual named The One Who Is The One.
3. And my parents are wanted for treason. And we still

have no idea where they are, or whether they are still alive.

4. We were tortured in a "magic-dampening" prison. So possibly we're more powerful than we even know.

5. A dead girl—who just happens to be the true love of my brother's young life—showed up mysteriously and rescued us from prison.

6. I turned Byron Swain into a weasel. *That,* I'm very proud of.

7. The world is actually plural, not singular. Between the Shadowland, Freeland, Overworld, and Underworld, it's hard not to lose count.

8. And one of those worlds is being run by a bunch of kids…from the manager's desk in a semidemolished department store. It isn't paradise, but at least it's a place where freedom still reigns.

9. I am being asked to help orchestrate a prison raid that might save kids from being vaporized. But maybe not. Actually, it might get all of them killed.

Okay, so it was a lot to deal with, but sometimes a list can really help you get a handle on life. "One thing at a time" is one of the more helpful philosophies.

Next week was next week. Right now, number nine was what mattered to everyone around Whit and me.

But we were still hung up on number three.

Chapter 67

Wisty

"SO, ABOUT THIS RAID. It's tomorrow?" I asked. "At the Overworld Prison? Do you know how the jail's laid out? Not that I'm committing Whit or myself. I can't do that."

Janine quickly punched a few keys, and the computer screen showed a schematic of a building. Byron Hateful Tattling Rat-Faced Weasel Swain leaped from Feffer and scampered up my back to sit on my shoulder so he could see.

I spun my head his way. "Quit climbing on me, or I'll switch on my flames and turn you into the world's grossest shish kebab," I told him. "That's all we need now, a double-crossing weasel spy, telling the New Order all our plans."

Byron slunk back down to the floor. "I won't!" he protested, cringing. "Never. Won't happen."

Janine blinked. "The weasel is a spy? It's a *talking* weasel?"

"Long story," I said. "But I don't trust this weasel as far as I can throw him, which I guess would be about thirty feet," I mused, looking at him. "How much do you weigh now?"

"I'm not a spy!" Byron said. "You think I could go back to them? Looking like this? I could have the secret of the universe, and they would still execute me in half a sec."

"All the same, you go out there. Go!" I said firmly, pointing to the hallway.

Looking insulted and hurt, Byron huffed and scuttled across the floor.

I turned back to the jail schematic. "Okay, what's the plan to save those kids again? You *do* have a plan?"

Chapter 68

Wisty

"FIRST, AS BACKGROUND, we need to give you a quick tour of the New Order's first stronghold," said Janine. "They call it the City of Progress because it's their ideal community. It's kind of the floor model for what they want to carpet the entire planet with. The place is full of erlenmeyers."

She put two fingers in her mouth and let out an ear-splitting whistle. A couple of guys came running.

Janine nodded to the tall, skinny, very clean-cut one. "Jonathan will take you on the tour. But first, Emmet will help with your disguises."

"Disguises?" Whit said.

"Absolutely," Janine insisted. "You need to blend in— you can't look too pukka. Otherwise, you know—*off with your heads!*"

Emmet, a very good-looking blond guy, said, "Come

on! First, we go to Cosmetics. I'll do your makeup. Don't worry—I'm *very* good."

An hour or so later, my totally uncontrollable hair was shiny and brushed, and kept off my face with an ingeniously placed hair bow and about two dozen hidden bobby pins. My clothes were country-club pink and lime green, rather than the usual black and grays that I favor.

Byron Unctuous Weasel had climbed on the filing cabinet. Now he looked me up and down with his beady little eyes.

"You look very nice," he said. "Actually, I approve."

I stuck my tongue out at him as Whit came strolling up to me. His face was pinkish and scrubbed, his hair was cut short—shorter than usual, even—and he looked cleaner than he had in a long time. If I weren't his sister, I might have even called him handsome. But since I *am* his sister, I said, "Why, hello, sir, I don't think we've met. I'm Wisty the Wicked Witch. And you?"

"Um, poster boy for the National Guard."

Feffer came over and sniffed around to make sure I was still me, and Whit was really Whit. We both passed and got licks.

"Okay," said Jonathan, coming up to us. He really was tall, several inches over even Whit. But he probably weighed about as much as I did. With his pale skin and fair, sandy hair, he resembled a bar of white chocolate.

"A few key things to remember: First and foremost, no cantrips. Don't talk to anyone unless you must. If you have to speak, remember to smile and say 'ma'am' or 'sir.' Do *not* cross the street against the light, do *not* snap gum in public, and for God's sake, do *not* let that dog do her business. All dogs in the City of Progress are trained to use litter boxes indoors, like cats."

"Sounds like a neat place," Whit muttered. "And what's a 'cantrip'?"

"No funny witchy stuff," Jonathan declared. "Okay, let's go meet the enemy!"

Chapter 69

Wisty

WHAT I NOTICED most about the City of Progress was that The One Who Is The One was, quite literally, every-where — on posters, paintings, videos, front pages of news-papers, murals. Who *was* this wackjob? I thought people like him came to power only in other places, in history books, in fantasy stories.

Until now, I never noticed how much fantasy had to do with reality.

What I noticed next about the City of Progress was fresh paint. You couldn't get away from the smell. Every-thing was so tidy and perfect. There weren't many kids around either, and when we saw grown-ups, they checked us out. Whit and I learned to copy Jonathan's quick smile.

We saw signs of the new regime everywhere: bumper stickers on the bright, shiny SUVs and minivans saying things like SAY YES TO THE N.O. and IF YOU SEE SOMETHING, SAY SOMETHING. And JUST SAY NO TO ART! Or, the most scary of the bunch in my opinion, PROUD PARENT OF A NEW ORDER JUNIOR INFORMANT.

"Oh *goodness*," I said, spying a low, chrome-trimmed building and immediately feeling weak in the knees. "A diner!" The idea of having some comfort food almost made me whimper. "Would it be safe to go in there? Please?"

"Yeah, I guess," said Jonathan. "Just remember your manners. Think 'New Order.'"

Inside the diner, almost every red-vinyl booth was occupied by grown-ups. A guy in a bleached cap was wiping down a glaringly white counter, over and over and over. We sat down on revolving stools in front of him. My stomach growled, which was more than a little embarrassing.

"Yes?" the counterman asked. "Help you folks?"

"Gosh, mister, it's hard to decide," I said, trying to radiate Tattling Weaselness and Jonathanness as best as I could. "May I please have a root-beer float and the cheeseburger deluxe? Thank you."

"Wisty," Whit said in a low voice, leaning in close, his breath warm on my ear, "do you feel something...*odd*? Because I sure do."

Very casually, I spun on my revolving stool.

I glanced around, but all I saw were people chowing down on burgers, fries, and milk shakes. The New Order anthem—a drone of rigid drumbeats awkwardly mixed with a wailing emo diva—was playing on the jukebox. *Ew.* You know things have gotten bad when military marches pass for pop music.

Then one particular woman caught my eye. Lots of mascara, very big hair. She gave me a weird look. Then she turned back to the other folks at her booth. Two middle-aged women with way too much face paint, and also big hair.

"Yes," I whispered. "The one with a spool of spidery hair. Two others just like her. They're watching us."

"She's a witch," I heard a voice say then. I froze in midrevolution on my stool. The tiny hairs on my arms stood up like New Age troopers.

The counterman looked up from his obsessive cleaning and frowned as if a shot had been fired.

"What did you say, Mrs. Highsmith?" he asked.

"That obnoxiously red-haired girl there. She's a witch," said Mrs. Highsmith more forcefully. It was the same woman who'd been looking at me. "And that blond boy—the handsome one—there's something not right about him either!"

She could tell I was a witch—because *she* was one too.

Chapter 70

Wisty

"TAKES ONE TO KNOW ONE," I retorted.

Actually, I didn't say that at all. I'd learned a thing or two about controlling myself since being arrested and sentenced to death. So I made my eyes go circular and wide and did some of the best acting of my life.

"Where?" I gasped, spinning on my stool. I searched up and down the diner, looking fearfully at everyone.

"My sister's certainly *not* a witch!" said Whit, looking convincingly astonished. Hunks are great at that, especially sincere ones — trust me. I've been living with Whit's act since I was an infant.

"This girl was just named Sector Leader's Star of Honor," Jonathan said. He was pretty good too.

"Maybe . . . maybe Mrs. Highsmith is imagining things?" I said. "Maybe she . . . *sees* things? Is that possible? Hmm? Mrs. Highsmith, do you have visions?"

Now all eyes were on the woman and her shady lady

friends. She flushed bright red. "Just *test* her!" she said in a loud, shrill voice.

"I'd be happy to take a test," I said quickly. "If *you* take one too."

Everyone was real quiet, waiting to see what she'd do next. All of a sudden, anger washed over me. If she knew what it meant to be different, why would she persecute others like herself?

"It's not me, *it's her!*" said Mrs. Highsmith.

Now people in the diner were starting to murmur, clearly suspicious.

In my mind, I conjured up a picture of her table. I saw her metal fork, where it rested on the napkin by her plate.

"My dad says not to talk to people like her," Jonathan said, sliding off his stool and backing toward the door. Whit and I got up too. "Come on, guys. We're done here. Let's report this place."

In the next half second, I *saw* her fork, *felt* it, and *knew* in my mind what I needed to do with it.

Which is why the fork rose up off the table and zipped through the air—*right at my face.*

"Help!" I shrieked, throwing up my hands. "Somebody help me! Please!"

The fork struck the back of my hand, harder than I'd intended, actually. I screeched, which worked to perfect effect. The patrons of the diner broke into a full-voiced uproar of shock and disapproval.

"Why is she trying to hurt me?" I squealed. "How did

she do that? That's unnatural! She stabbed me with her fork! *It flew!*"

"Call Security Services!" someone got up and shouted. "She hurt that Star of Honor girl. She *is* a witch."

"It's not me, it's *her!*" Mrs. Highsmith screamed again as the crowd moved toward her.

For the first time, I felt just the littlest, tiniest bit guilty about my powers.

I mean, maybe she was simply a helpless, grumpy old lady.

But I sure doubted it!

Chapter 71

Wisty

THE COUNTERMAN QUICKLY examined some kind of chart—like the ones normally posted for how to rescue a choking victim—and yelled, "Pin her arms tightly enough to cut off the circulation, then gag her so she can't cast any more spells!"

Meanwhile we eased out the front door, casting nervous glances behind us at every single step. Sirens were wailing our way, racing closer and closer.

I could see Mrs. Highsmith pinned up against the plateglass window, at least a dozen paper napkins wedged in her mouth as an impromptu gag. I actually felt sorry for her.

Then the old woman spied me watching. She stared at me balefully for a moment and then began to *glow*—like I had that time at the Hospital. I felt somewhat relieved. My instincts were right: she really was a witch.

Then she did the unexpected: I saw her wave one hand for us to go. Was she on our side?

It got even better. Her citizen attackers floated up in the air like life-size balloons. Then they were thrown back, away from her and her witch friends, cartwheeling and somersaulting into the depths of the diner, screeching, "Help us, help us!"

Keeping her eyes locked on me, she casually pulled the napkins from her mouth. Her friends continued to calmly munch their sandwiches and sip tea. Then it was the weirdest thing—she pointed with her right hand, but only the gnarled index finger and pinkie, like she was flashing me a sign.

Or maybe putting a curse on me? What was *that* all about?

And then she and her antique girlfriends *disappeared*. Poof, gone.

"A coven," I whispered to Whit. "That was a coven of witches."

Chapter 72

Whit

THE NIGHT OF the Mrs. Highsmith incident, we all slept in the Bed and Bath Department at Garfunkel's, hoping we hadn't been cursed and wouldn't wake up as toads. Bet you didn't know you could fit two teenagers, a large dog, and a traitorous weasel into one double bed. Of course, it helps if one of the kids floats a couple of feet above the mattress during her dream cycles.

Still, some of the king-size beds near us had as many as six or seven kids sleeping on them. There were hundreds of us in the store. On mattresses, in sleeping bags, on piles of couch cushions, rolled up in bedding and bath towels. It was like a counselor-free, postapocalyptic summer camp. The relief at being out of the Hospital and away from the Matron, the Visitor, Judge Ezekiel Unger, and the New Order's nightmare regime made it all seem positively homey.

The next morning, I was looking at myself in a mirror

outside the men's dressing rooms. I'd found a set of free weights down in Sporting Goods and seen how much of a feeb I'd gotten to be in jail. I began working out again, building my strength, knowing I would need it eventually.

"*Ahem.*" A cough behind me made me jump. "Wizard All-good." It was Janine. "I have someone I'd like you to meet."

As usual, cute as Janine was, she was as solemn-faced as a vice principal. The girl next to her, however, was grinning. She was maybe sixteen or seventeen, dark-skinned, on the short side, but probably weighed two hundred pounds.

"Hi," she said, sticking out her hand. "I'm Jamilla. I'm the shaman."

"The huh?" I said, shaking her hand anyway. I noticed how her brown eyes shone and her wild corkscrew hair made a fluffy wedge up and away from her face.

"The shaman," Jamilla repeated. "In other words, another oddball. Kind of like you and your sister, only I don't do magic myself. I just help *other people* do cantrips. Been working with a few witches and wizards, helping them hone their powers."

"Hi," said Wisty, joining us. "We know we have special powers—but sometimes they're hard to control. Most of the time, actually."

"It's hard to master one's magical endowments," Jamilla reassured us. "We're finding there's a range, from people who know who's calling on the phone to a few who can actually make small objects float in the air. Some can even say what's in your pockets or purse."

Jamilla smiled and raised her eyebrows to show how impressed she was with that.

Wisty and I exchanged glances. "We hear you."

"But I'm curious to find out what you two can do. We've never seen the New Order spend such resources and time on anybody before. I mean, our sources tell us that they fitted that entire crazy-house mingus with magic-dampening materials just for you two."

"I guess we should be flattered," I said dryly. "But it's like Wisty said—we can do some magic, but it's hard to control."

"Like what?" Jamilla said eagerly. Some other kids were starting to gather around us now.

"Well, like this," said Wisty, and she burst into flames.

Everyone started screaming and backing away, even the shaman.

"Show-off," I said.

Chapter 73

Whit

MY SISTER JUST STOOD THERE, four-feet-long flames whipping out and away from her, her eyes blinking, unconcerned, in her fiery face. As you might imagine, everyone was shrieking like, well, kids watching somebody on fire. Before I even had a chance to figure out how to smother the flames, her fire went out.

"*I did it!*" Wisty punched the air with her fist. "I put myself out!"

"High five, sister!" I cheered. "You the witch!"

Jamilla looked a little sick. "Did you do that *on purpose?*" she asked hoarsely.

"Yeah, totally," said Wisty. "Usually, though, it happens by accident, like if I'm really mad. But that was the first time I've been able to start and stop the fire on my own. Normally somebody has to get me really ticked off—and then get a fire extinguisher."

Jamilla gave a low whistle of amazement. "What else can you do?"

"She floated," said a boy who couldn't have been more than five. He pointed at Wisty. "I saw her do it. She floated last night. Like a balloon over the bed."

"Oh yeah," said Wisty, embarrassed. "Sometimes I do that. Not intentionally."

I heard gasping and murmuring from the crowd.

"Whit stuck his hand through a wall," Wisty said. "And stopped a gavel in midair. And I threw a fork at myself—long story—and froze a bunch of guard dogs at the Hospital."

"You . . . fro—," said Jamilla faintly.

"I *un*froze them too," Wisty said defensively. "I didn't leave them that way. I couldn't do that to dogs. Ask Feffer. And I glow sometimes, kind of like that witch in town did right before she sent all those people flying in the diner. Don't know what that's about yet."

Everyone might have been a lot more skeptical, but they'd just seen a human flamesicle.

"The leeches," I remembered, nodding.

"Oh yeah," said Wisty. "I made a bunch of horseflies, even though I was trying to make a giant cockroach." She shuddered.

"And then there's little ole me," said a voice down by our feet.

"Your talking weasel?" said Janine.

"He wasn't always a weasel," Wisty admitted. "But this is his true form."

212

"My true form was the lion," he squeaked.

"That was probably your *opposite* form," said Wisty, glaring menacingly at Byron, who glared right back.

"Oh my God," Jamilla said, looking from us to Janine. Janine's eyes widened.

"You think?" she said to the shaman.

"Janine, I think this is them!"

"Them who?" I asked. "Them what?" Did I really want to hear this?

"The Liberators," Jamilla blurted, still staring at us. "The Rescuers. Check this out. There's a prophecy—and *it's about the two of you.*"

Chapter 74

Whit

JAMILLA TURNED AND RAN to a nearby wall on the way to the gift-wrap counter. Her puffy hair was bouncing around like a Slinky. The wall had velvet rope in front of it to keep people away, but Jamilla stepped right over it.

"This here is the Prophecy Wall. Sometimes messages appear on it. Usually it's just store stuff, like *Huge white sale in January.* But sometimes it's *Go to Fifth Street. Rescue an orphan kid from house number twenty-four,* things like that. A while ago, it predicted two Liberators who possessed magic would come to help overthrow the New Order. So, my friends, you must be the real deal, you know what I'm saying?"

She turned to the group of people who had followed us to the wall. "Does anyone here think this is just a coincidence? Anyone? *Anyone?*"

Suddenly everybody started clapping and cheering wildly. Everybody but Wisty and me, that is.

"Huh," I said. It was just a wall, *a blank wall*. Was that

the latest and greatest prophecy? *Nada?* Nothing? Meaning either we were about to slip into a void or, almost as grim, nothing was going to change?

"No, really, the message was there," said Jamilla. "Wait a few seconds. It doesn't always do it."

We stared at the plain wall, a slice of textured wallpaper curling down from one corner. Very unremarkable . . .

Wisty looked at me, and I shrugged big-time.

"Well, it comes and goes," said Janine, pushing back her hair. "But we've all seen it." Various heads in the crowd nodded.

Okeydoke. Maybe the wall was just out of prophecies today.

"Even if you're right," I said, "how are we supposed to overthrow a government powerful enough to destroy entire cities and build new ones? Besides, we're still going to look for our mother and father."

"We told you that from the beginning," said Wisty.

"Look!" someone said, and I turned to the Prophecy Wall again. This time I saw letters forming. *What the . . . ?*

ONE DAY SOON, KIDS WILL RUN THE WORLD . . .

A shiver ran through me. I had heard similar words before—from Celia. The message continued:

. . . AND DO A BETTER JOB THAN THE
GROWN-UPS EVER DID.

"Whoa," Wisty murmured. "Heavy."

Suddenly Sasha came running up to Janine and whispered something in her ear. Janine listened, nodded, and seemed to get flustered—especially for her.

She looked at Wisty and me. "Sasha, tell them," she said. "Go ahead."

"We've just gotten a message from our spies monitoring the Overworld Prison. More exterminations are scheduled for tomorrow morning. Vaporization."

There were gasps and horrified murmurs around the room, and after hearing Michael Clancy's story, I had the same reaction. So did Wisty.

"But there's something else," Sasha said, and he looked directly at the two of us. "Your parents have been captured again."

"*What?*" Wisty and I shouted.

"Where are they?" Wisty demanded to know.

"Wherever they are, we're there," I announced, "effective immediately. Sorry we can't help you guys, Sasha."

"No need to apologize," he reassured me confidently. "In fact, your parents are being held at Overworld."

I didn't even need to look at Wisty to know what she was thinking. The word "vaporization" was pounding in our brains.

"That being the case—," I began.

"We're in," Wisty said without missing a beat.

Chapter 75

Wisty

THE TEAM LEADER for the break-in at the Overworld Prison was a girl, which I loved. Her name was Margo, and although she was about my size, she was as tough as razor blades. She had to be—she'd already escaped from Overworld, and lost a couple of fingers. She was also homicidal when it came to The One Who Is The One.

And I have to admit I was starting to be too. He intended to vaporize my parents tomorrow, after all. We wouldn't let that happen.

Margo led the way through an abandoned subway station that was dank and dark, but we had flashlights from the hardware section at Garfunkel's.

"Once we get inside, we should let the kids out first, since we know where they are. Then we can go looking for your parents," said Margo.

"Let's wait and see, okay?" recommended Whit. "Once

we get inside, we'll make a final plan. But that raises the big question, doesn't it: how do we break into Overworld?"

Margo looked at the two of us. "Magic would be good."

Whit and I stopped walking, and then so did the rest of our band of nine.

"There's no real plan to get inside, is there?" Whit asked.

"We can always get ourselves arrested," Margo said. "That shouldn't be a big problem."

I'd been half listening to them, but mostly I was thinking about seeing our mother and father again, and I couldn't wait. Now it was time to get down to business.

"I have a plan," I said. "I've been going over it a lot. First, we need disguises, of course, ones that allow us to blend with the prison environment. I was thinking that Whit could be a guard. I can try to make him look older and give him a guard's uniform. Then he can just walk in. I don't want to be arrested again, Margo."

"So what about you?" Whit asked me. "How do you get in, Wisty?"

"It has to be magic that I can do. Consistently. So I tried some things before we left Garfunkel's. I can do something fairly interesting that I think'll work."

"Do *what?*" Whit asked.

"You're going to think it's stupid. And crazy."

"Wisty, what are you going to do? How do you get inside?"

"Well, I..." Wisty paused, then blurted out the rest. "*Turnmyselfintoamouse.*"

218

Chapter 76

Wisty

"A MOUSE?" Whit looked like he might explode. "A *mouse?* You're going in there disguised as a *rodent?* To rescue Mom and Dad, and all those kids? And maybe tangle with The One Who Is The One?"

I nodded. "A mouse can go places without anyone seeing. A mouse can chew through wires or sneak through skinny pipes. A mouse can do things even an elephant can't do," I pointed out.

"A mouse can also get squashed by some guard's boot. Or vaporized. *No,*" said Whit. "It's too dangerous. And *it's nuts.*"

I refused to back off my idea, because it was a good one. I was sure of it. "But it'll also give me a chance to go places that no one else can go. I can do this, Whit. I tried snakes, roaches, bats—I can do a mouse. And," I said with a half smile, "I have a good track record with small animals, right?"

There was a very uncomfortable silence for a few seconds while everyone digested my plan, such as it was. In the meantime, we'd made it out of the subway and were up on a street, though we stayed in the shadows.

"I don't like it," Whit said, but I could tell he was weakening.

"Trust me," I said. "I'm a witch. Watch this. Watch very closely."

Chapter 77

Wisty

I WHIPPED OUT my drumstick like it was a six-gun and — get this — it *crackled*. This time my magic worked like it was supposed to. I started by making Whit look older, and put him in a guard's uniform that was perfect to the last detail, with the New Order logo and everything.

Next, I snapped the drumstick at myself, and everybody gasped. One of the kids almost fainted on the spot.

"I hope you're right about this," Whit said, pulling his guard's cap down tight over his forehead. "I have my doubts at the moment."

Margo, who was a logic-police kind of gal, just shook her head in dismay.

I had to admit, looking at my handiwork — Whit in his guard uniform, a dead ringer for a guy in his thirties — that I was getting much better at my craft.

Not to mention that I'd managed to turn myself into *vermin*.

I hadn't realized how weeny mice were. I was now about the size of a large fig, covered everywhere with white-and-brown glossy fur. I had long white whiskers that tickled my face and ears that were hair-trigger twitchy.

I whipped my tail around my side and caught sight of it. *Okay, that's pretty cool! Makes up for the embarrassing ear-twitch tic.*

Whit showed me my reflection in his regulation New Order silver belt buckle, and I had to admit, I made a cute enough mouse, as far as mice go. And a very promising witch.

But then I looked up and down the street where we were, and my confidence flagged. Imagine, if you will, a fast-moving car tire that seemed the size of an elephant on steroids, or a lumbering human being the size of a rocket-ship. I never realized how traumatized your average mouse must be. *It may take me years of therapy to get over this....*

"What time is it?" Emmet whispered.

"Five minutes to seven," Margo answered. "We've got two blocks to go. Come on! This is it. Shift change."

"Margo," I said, "pick up my drumstick, and please, please, keep it safe." She reached and grabbed the stick where it had fallen when I no longer had hands to hold it.

Next, I looked up at Whit. "Put me in your pocket," I said.

Chapter 78

Wisty

I DIDN'T LIKE IT one bit inside Whit's pocket, especially once he started to run. It was like being on a boat in a rough sea: up and down and up and down. Within a block I felt myself going green, and I half wondered if there was a spell I could mutter for mouse-size motion-sickness pills. It would not be cool to barf in my brother's trousers.

"There's the van with the new prisoners," Whit said. "Same one we came in."

"Hurry!" Margo urged.

We sped up, the horrible rocking motion of Whit's powerful stride making me moan and close my eyes.

Then he reached into his pocket and plucked me out so I could see. We had gotten to the prison gates just as the van pulled up and honked.

"Go," Emmet told Whit. My brother tossed something into a wire trash can near the street corner. With a soft *floom*, the contents of the can turned into a giant fire.

"What's that? What happened?" Whit cried, pointing at the trash.

Immediately the gate guards leaped into action, racing down the street, leaving the van and its driver for a precious moment. The driver entered a code on a pad, and the high metal gates began to open. Whit slipped inside, staying just out of the man's view.

Once we were within the gates, my nose twitched uncontrollably. The odor seemed like it was piped in from the Hospital.

For a moment, I couldn't bear the idea of facing it again. And then I remembered my parents and knew there was no turning back.

The driver opened the van doors, and a lot of scared kids slowly climbed out, looking around with saucer-wide eyes. A guard stepped out of the inner gatehouse, ready to process the new prisoners, some of them no more than five or six. I felt sick at the thought of what horrors were in store for these innocent kids.

Whit and I locked eyes—and yes, I swear that a mouse and a human can actually do this—and we each whispered the identical words that we'd practiced:

Sleep now, little ones,
    Rest your heads and sleep.
The night will hold you in its arms,
    And safely you will keep.

Our mother and father had sung this lullaby to us when we were little, and I hadn't been able to remember a single thing past the last word because I'd always dropped like a stone into sleep when they'd finished. Whit and I were banking on the fact that they'd actually been using magic to put their totally wired kids to bed at night.

Okay, so it was a stretch.

And, sure enough, *nothing happened.*

The guard and the driver talked nonchalantly and flipped papers on their clipboards, chatting, just another day incarcerating innocent children, la-di-da. Whit and I looked at each other, and I saw panic starting in his eyes.

Sleep, you goons, sleep! I thought desperately, wishing I had my drumstick and hoping I wasn't going to end up as mouse paste in the next few seconds.

The gates slammed shut behind us, our friends locked outside the prison, and here we were, a fake guard who might turn back into a teenager at any second, a mouse who might turn back into a girl at any second, and two New Order goons who were going to notice that something strange was going on and sound the alarm.

Any second now.

Chapter 79

Wisty

PEERING OVER WHIT'S curled index finger, I saw the humongous men slowly turn to look at my brother. One of them wrinkled his brow.

"You're new here, aren't you?" he asked Whit. "Haven't seen you around before. What's your name, bub?"

You. Will. Sleep. Now! I thundered the words. *Inside* my head, of course. *YOU. WILL. SLEEP. NOW!*

(I figured all CAPS and italics had to work.)

And then . . . the two men crumpled to the pavement at Whit's feet. Dead asleep. Gonzo to the worldo.

The kid prisoners stared at the goons with alarm, as if maybe they were next to go la-la.

"It's okay," Whit told them. "We're your friends. You have to trust us, okay? We're *kids*."

Then Whit held me up close to his face. "Are you sure about this?" he whispered. "This isn't a game, Wisty."

"Whit, there's no turning back now. Mom and Dad, and all those kids who could be turned into smoke and ash, are inside. Get these new kids in the van and get them out of here. Pick up Margo and Emmet. Tell them to stay close by. If I can disarm the alarm or the gate, they'll have to shuttle the escaping kids through the tunnels *really* fast."

Whit frowned, and it was so weird—even the creases in his skin looked huge. Even his one zit. "If you see chunks of cheese or peanut butter, like, lying in the middle of a small wooden board, with wire all around it—"

"I got it," I said. "Drag those sleeping guys into the gatehouse."

Whit let out a breath, looking extremely unhappy with me. "We'll all be standing by. I'll be watching for you, Wisteria." Which, he knew, was what Dad always called me in times of great stress.

"Okay," I said. I stared down at the ground, which looked about ten stories away. I closed my eyes and jumped, quite pleasantly surprised when I landed neatly on all fours, ready to run. "See, I didn't go splat!" I called to Whit.

"You be careful!" he called back.

"'Careful' is my middle name!" I looked ahead at the very large, gray prison building. Right away I saw a drainpipe and headed over to it. Before I actually entered the pipe, I glanced back at my brother, trying not to think this might be the last time I'd ever see him.

"See ya," I called in a voice he couldn't possibly hear.

Then I peered up into the darkness of the rusty pipe. I could smell damp air, old leaves, and other nasty things I couldn't identify. I'd heard mice were excellent climbers.

I guess I was about to find out.

Chapter 80

Whit

I SHUDDERED AND CRINGED as I watched Wisty's tiny tail corkscrew, then disappear, up that drainpipe. No magic could wipe away the grotesque image of her being crushed under a New Order prison guard's jackboot.

But my job now was to save the kids who'd just been brought in the van, and then I could get to my parents. The quicker, the better.

"We're not staying here?" one of them asked timidly as I backed the vehicle out of the gates. "Isn't that against the New Order rules?"

"No to your first question, yep to the second," I said, making sure there was no oncoming traffic. "Change of plans. It's all good."

I popped the truck into drive and swung out into the street fast, racing to the alley we'd passed on our way in. I rolled down my window and waved.

Margo, Emmet, and the others emerged from the shadows.

"Where's Wisty?" Margo asked.

"Up a drainpipe. Where else?" I said. "We have to ditch this van."

"No! We can use it later," said Emmet, sitting beside me in the front seat. Margo crammed herself in too. "Go up three blocks and take a right at the light."

Margo reassured the kids as we drove. "You aren't criminals. We're taking you to live with us. It isn't fancy, but it's better than prison."

"We're not going to jail?" one girl asked, wiping her tear-streaked cheeks with both hands.

"No," said Margo, "we're going to Garfunkel's."

Seeing their little faces relax was incredible, I must admit. I knew they'd have lots of questions, but at least they had hope. They had us.

"This next part gets a little tricky," Emmet said nervously. "But it'll get us back to Garfunkel's without being seen on the main streets."

"Oh no, not *that*," Margo yelped, looking alarmed—okay, make that *frightened*. "It's a death trap!"

"It's the only way!" Emmet said.

"Uh, can we go back to the death-trap part?" I asked.

"Right *here!*" Emmet shouted suddenly, grabbing the wheel. "Sharp left!"

"There's nothing there!" I shouted back as the van hopped the curb.

"Hang on, everybody!" Margo commanded. "This could get a little rough!"

I whipped my head from side to side, checking for innocent pedestrians I should avoid mowing down.

"There!" Emmet said, pointing again.

"Where?"

Then I saw what he meant . . . too late.

Chapter 81

Whit

I SLAMMED ON THE BRAKES, but apparently if you're driving a heavy van full of kids and you're suddenly on a steep *staircase* going *down*, the brakes give out immediately.

The children in back screamed like they were strapped into a thrill ride built by a serial killer. I had a split second to wonder if they all wished they were back at the prison, getting little gray-striped jumpsuits to try on.

But that was the only coherent thought I managed before we were bouncing around too much to think straight.

Down, down, down!

Gachonk, gachonk, gachonk!

Why is it that time flies when you're having fun, but when you're behind the wheel, plummeting down a flight of steps in a van full of hysterical kids, time virtually stops? The laws of physics are *so* unfair.

"What were you thinking?" I yelled at Emmet. "This is a subway station!"

"That's right!" Emmet shouted over the *gachonking* noise of the crunching shock absorbers—which didn't seem to be absorbing too much shock. The sound of the kids' screaming bounced up and down like hysterical hiccups. "Another abandoned subway! We can ride the tracks all the way to the portal, which will bring us home!"

Oh, no way, I thought as the van got a couple of huge jolts—smashing through the turnstiles—then bounced across a platform and skidded sideways in horribly slow motion... toward the edge.

Everyone shrieked in panic as the van skittered along the platform's lip for a few long, agonizing seconds before dropping like a ton of concrete right onto the subway tracks.

Silence rushed in to fill the void where the *non-amusement-park-ride* screaming had been. I felt like someone had just taken us out of one of those paint-can shakers at the hardware store.

We were right smack on the tracks of the subway, though, our now cockeyed headlights shining into cavernous darkness. I turned the van off and stared at Emmet.

"There we go. No problem," he said finally, his voice a little shaky in the crushing silence. His face was also whiter than a marble statue's.

"Everyone okay?" I croaked.

"Let's not do that again," one of the kids said through tears. "Okay, mister?"

"The worst part's over," said Emmet. "Now we can ride

these rails without anyone looking for the van or any of you missing prisoners. A turnoff tunnel will take us right to the portal."

A long, low whistle suddenly echoed through the blackness.

"Another train, far away," said Emmet. "Okay, let's get a move on."

I reflexively checked the rearview mirror as I felt for the ignition key under the steering wheel.

What I saw was a bright, single light piercing the darkness behind us.

"Um, *not* so far away." I turned to Emmet, my heart slamming into my chest.

"What?" asked Emmet.

"Take a look out the back window."

He didn't need to. The kids' screams told him everything he needed to know.

Chapter 82

Wisty

IF YOU'RE EVER on the brink of death—or, in my case, of ill-fated eternal life as a rodent—I recommend singing childhood songs to lift your spirits. How can you be climbing up a drainpipe without indulging in a cheerful round of "Itsy Bitsy Spider"? I sang the line about the spider being *washed out* with a nervous titter as I ascended into the prison complex.

From the drainpipe, I came out into a gutter. I raced along the roof edge until I found an air-conditioning vent, just like I'd seen in the prison schematic back at Janine's computer.

Excellent. I squeezed through and then ran along the duct until I found another vent. And then another. And another.

I was as close as I ever wanted to being a rat in a maze.

But right then I was becoming increasingly aware of another mouse side effect: you can smell a million times better than you can as a person. I quickly found out that I could actually *follow my nose.* Pretty soon I came to a turn-off that I knew had to be the right one. It smelled like hell on a particularly hot day.

The conduit was completely dark, but I figured I'd be able to see better when my eyes adjusted. Or I could always set myself on fire. Almost snickering at the vision of a flaming rodent skittering through the prison, I stretched my neck in through the slats, then squeezed my body most of the way. One final heroic tug, and I was suddenly dropping down, down, *down,* into nothing.

Chapter 83

Wisty

THERE'S A GOOD REASON our worst nightmares are so often about falling. That deer-in-the-headlights awareness that something really, *really* bad's coming, but not being able to *do* anything about it, is probably the world's best (or should I say *worst?*) recipe for ultimate, deluxe, supersize terror.

I plunged headlong into the spinning, blurring darkness, bouncing off one dusty metal wall and then another, flailing in order to catch something—anything—to slow my descent.

But there was nothing. Just the wind blowing harder and harder as I fell faster and faster.

And faster.

And still there was no sign of the bottom. Although, in this pitch-dark shaft, I probably wouldn't even see it coming.

"STOP!" I squealed mindlessly. *Think fast, Wisty.* I was a witch. A witch could use magic. Magic could stop a falling object. Whit stopped a gavel in midair. Why couldn't I stop something as small and light as a mouse?

I gestured with my paws, I flicked my tail like a wand, I wished and raged the way I had in the past when I'd gone invisible or burst into flames...but nothing worked. I felt about as magical as a tomato. A tomato dropping from the roof of a very tall building.

About to go *splat!*

I have to say, the old cliché about your life flashing before your very eyes is dead-on. I saw it all: Wisty, the feisty but loving daughter. Wisty, the high school truant. Wisty, the bad, scary witch. Wisty, the Liberator. Wisty, the Roadkill. Or something that was about to look a lot like it anyway.

Then it hit me. Literally stopped my panicked breath. Not the force of a hard surface. Instead, I was clobbered by a rank *smell* that was about a hundred times worse than Whit's gym bag.

And I was falling right toward it.

A dim light began to fill the tube below me, and in an instant I saw where my free fall would come to an end: in the prison garbage pile.

Luckily, a mesh screen was fastened across the opening to the shaft. I hit it at what felt like sixty miles an hour. It's a good thing the wire had some give to it, or I'm sure I would have been flattened on the spot. If the screen had been tighter or any thinner, it might have passed through me like an apple corer.

As it was, the thing worked like an overstretched trampoline and sent me rebounding back up into the vent before my final smackdown.

The force of the impact knocked the wind out of me, and I was instantly sure I'd broken some ribs and my left foreleg. Judging from how my head was throbbing and the fact that I couldn't see straight, I probably had a concussion too.

Shaken, injured, disoriented, but alive, I forced myself to scan my surroundings. I'd made a serious dent in the screen, and the rusty old clasps that held the thing in place had nearly bent straight.

Then I recoiled at the sound of some squeaky chattering below me. I choked back my vertigo—I'm so bad about heights I usually turn around and face upward on down escalators—then rolled over and peered through the screen.

It wasn't technically a trash pit but an open-topped steel container, filled with torn bedding, soiled inmate uniforms, and revolting scraps from the prison kitchen. And—wait—it was full of *eyes* staring right at me!

Rats. Dozens of them. Filthy-furred, greasy-tailed, evil-looking.

I'm not especially squeamish about them normally. My science teacher even had one in the classroom last year. But these weren't nice white pet-store rats like Mr. Nicolo's. And I wasn't a human girl here. I was a mouse—aka *prey.*

Come on, magic. Come on. A spell to let me climb or fly? A spell to let me banish rats to oblivion? A spell to turn me into a large cat? A spell to make this all into a dream I could wake up from?

But my mind, my energy, my spirit, were stone-cold frozen. All I could manage was to stare back at the rats—at their matted fur, their soulless black eyes, their wicked yellow teeth, their wormy pink tails.

I was safe for the moment. There was at least eight feet of space between me and them, and unless they were really good with cheerleader-squad pyramids, they wouldn't be able to get anywhere near me.

I looked up into the shaft and spied a ridge, a seam in the metal where two sections had been welded together. It wasn't much, but it might be enough to grip. And if there was another seam above that, and another above that...

I jumped desperately upward, my good foreleg outstretched, and missed.

And that was too bad, because the clasps on the screen really weren't ready for me to fall on them again, and they promptly gave way.

No, no, *no!*

The screen swung open and I fell backward, helplessly airborne once again, plunging toward the trash and the nightmare scrum of rats.

Chapter 84

Wisty

I THINK WE ALL CAN recognize that rats are not the cutest animals in the world. But until you're one-tenth their size, you don't really have a good sense of just how unsavory they are. To be as up close to them as I was right then...well, personally I'd rather face a tiger or a grizzly bear.

At least tigers and bears don't nest in trash heaps. These prison rodents smelled as if they'd give you an incurable disease just by brushing against you, to say nothing of what would happen if they sank their bone-splintering teeth into you.

They quickly circled around me as I landed on the heap and gasped for breath in the suffocating stink. There was no spark of mercy in their lightless eyes. And judging by the drool coming out of their crooked mouths, I was clearly *way* more appetizing than whatever moldy items they'd been finding in this revolting pile of rancid kitchen grease, soup bones, shredded uniforms, soaked mattress stuffing, rat droppings, and unidentifiable brown-and-black sludge.

Not wasting a moment to think about spells—or germs—I leaped at the largest gap in their circling pack and sprinted as fast as my aching body, and the slippery, treacherous sludge pile, would allow.

It was no use. Even beyond the first ring of rats, more were swarming. In a moment they had seized each of my legs and had pinned me down in the slimy pile.

A lean, fanged creature the size of a small wildcat loomed over me, snuffling my fur and drooling like I was a fresh-from-the-oven chocolate chip cookie...a treat for the Rat King.

I clenched my eyes shut and, well, screamed my fool head off.

And wouldn't you know it—right then, without any warning, I was sprouting like a charmed beanstalk in a fairy tale.

I'd become my full-size human self again!

Good news: the mouse spell must have worn off at just the right moment! And my human self wasn't all busted and broken. Bad news: maybe the last shred of magic I possessed had just evaporated. Good news: *Who freaking cares?* I just escaped death by dismemberment. And digestion.

And then more bad news: my transformation back into

human form had not been accompanied by a new wardrobe. There I was, lying in garbage, rats all over me, not a shred of clothing between me and them. I was *stark naked*.

A big pink rat chew toy.

But I'd suddenly become the largest creature in the trash, and the rats were pretty freaked out. They scurried up and over the top of the container.

I, in the meantime, quickly picked through the disgusting pile for an abandoned prisoner uniform to wear, and noticed the lettering on the back of each shirt:

NEW ORDER REFORMATORY
NO. 426

I finally found a uniform that fit and that wasn't entirely soaked through with sludge. I numbly put it on, nearly oblivious to its smell and sickening dampness.

There was a set of steel rungs at the front wall of the container, and—having never wanted anything more dearly than to be away from this rat-infested garbage pile—I climbed them faster than a bionic squirrel...and vowed to never make another rodent-based metaphor ever again.

Next I lowered myself out of the container to the floor and squinted around in the dimly lit indoor loading bay. I spotted the outline of a regular door atop a nearby loading dock and hurried to it.

It was unlocked, and I slowly pulled it open, allowing

my eyes to adjust to the bright fluorescent light beyond. It appeared to be a service corridor. Everything seemed quiet, so I cautiously stuck my head out into the hall.

I didn't do it cautiously enough, though. The six prison guards who had just turned the corner saw me right away.

Chapter 85

Wisty

I DIDN'T EVEN HAVE a split second to suck in a rejuvenating breath of non-stench-filled air before I had to take off running blindly like my life depended on it.

Which it did.

"Escapee!" one of the guards yelled as another slammed a red button on the wall, setting off earsplitting sirens and eye-shattering strobe lights.

As long as I didn't have control over my magic and was stuck in my enemy-friendly, easy-to-catch-and-destroy human form, I had about a 1 percent chance of survival. But I hung on to that 1 percent. Like crazy. It fueled me like a cheap sugar high. I wasn't going to do my parents any good if I got caught and killed.

I reached a stairwell and sprinted up two, three steps at a time. Made me wonder if I'd accidentally come back with longer legs in my mouse-to-Wisty morph. One flight, two flights, three flights, the boot steps behind me getting closer with every passing second. But I was still ahead.

Adrenaline rocks.

When I got to the last landing and the door to the roof, I heaved against the exit bar—and then I was out on top of the gravel-covered building. I bolted in the only direction that wasn't blocked by concertina wire.

"Stop right there! There's no escape!" I heard a meathead guard shout as he burst through the door behind me.

I skidded to a painful stop at the edge of a precipice that overlooked the central cell block's courtyard, a concrete parade area five stories below.

The guards knew they had me trapped. My only chance was to cross the courtyard gap on a two-foot-wide conduit—a metal round-backed pipe that stretched across the massive opening in the roof.

Anyone would be insane to try it. But *me?* Aside from the heights thing, balance and I don't have a good history. I'm serious. Ask Whit sometime about my one attempt at snowboarding.

Without turning to look at my pursuers, I carefully stepped out on the pipe and, arms pinwheeling, started across the pit.

"Stop and come back. You'll kill yourself!" yelled one of the guards, his tone not exactly overflowing with concern.

But I was already a quarter of the way across. I was making it!

It seemed like as long as I continued to move quickly, my momentum kind of kept me steady. And it probably helped that I was barefoot and the pipe was pitted with rust and not very slippery. I just kept my eyes focused on the far side of the pipe and made sure not to look down.

Which ended up being sort of a mistake, because a rope was fastened around the pipe at the halfway point. I failed to notice it.

I stubbed my toe, lost my balance, and fell into space.

Chapter 86

Whit

"THAT TRAIN IS COMING!" Emmet howled, swiveling nervously in his seat. *"Straight for us!* Fast, *really* fast!

"Get out of here, kids!" he shouted, grabbing for the door. "Leave the van! Immediately! Now, now, now!"

"No!" Margo yelled. "Drive, Whit! Stay put, everybody! Nobody moves! We have to outrun it. There's nowhere else for us to go!"

The van was actually starting to vibrate with the train's approach. I cranked the key and got a dull sputtering sound.

Attention, passengers: the train bound for Instantaneous Death is now approaching the platform on track one.

"I want to go back to prison!" I heard one of the kids cry out from the din of screaming and sobbing.

I cranked the engine again. Nothing happened.

Cold sweat broke out on my forehead—small, very distinct worry beads. The train's whistle swelled to a wail as the ground trembled. I tried to block out the screams.

I touched my hand to the key again.

Concentrate, I thought. *I have life in my hands. This energy must pass through me.... This van MUST go. THESE KIDS...MUST...LIVE!*

And then I did feel something coursing through me, unpleasant and weird, as if I'd stuck a wet finger in a light socket. My hands felt as if they were aflame as a physical force flew through my fingers and into the van's key.

I had to admit: I felt like...I was a wizard. Like I had superpowers. Like I was guilty as charged by The One Who Judges.

Suddenly the engine roared to life like it was the Lazarus of minivans.

Everyone went silent. A hopeful silence. Of course, we were still on the subway tracks with a train barreling down on us.

I slammed my foot down on the gas pedal. The wheels spun, spitting rocks and garbage out behind us. The train's headlight flooded our van, its horn so loud that it filled every inch of space inside my head.

And the van's wheels continued to churn in place. Hope, crushed.

Good-bye, Wisty, I thought. *So long, Mom and Dad.*

Then there was a lurching, the bottom of the vehicle screeching against the metal tracks. We surged forward.

Margo was shouting, "Go! Go! Go!"

"Thanks for the tip!" I shouted back.

Chapter 87

Wisty

THE ROPE I TRIPPED OVER also saved my life. It gave me a mean friction burn, but I managed to grab it as I plunged past the pipe. I quickly wrapped my legs around its downward-stretched length.

From there—given that my name's not Whit and I'm not exactly oversupplied with upper-body strength—climbing back up was out of the question. So I started sliding down, hopeful that the rope would take me close enough to the ground to jump off.

I heard a scuffle of boots and gooney guard voices shouting at one another from above. They'd witnessed my acrobatic feat and were heading back downstairs to tackle me from the courtyard.

This chase would be over if I didn't get there first.

I didn't even look down. I didn't want to see how far I had to fall—and also I didn't want to discover that I was going to run out of rope. Instead, I focused on the rows of cell-block window slits as I twisted my way down. Four stories to go, three stories to go, two stories to go —

But now my feet encountered something solid and cloth-covered, and I couldn't keep sliding on my merry way.

In hindsight, I wish I hadn't looked to see what it was. I wish I'd just jumped the remaining few yards to the ground and taken off running without a glance back. Because as I peered down, I saw that my feet were now resting on the sagging shoulders of *the Visitor*.

Or, at least, the shoulders of his bloated, long-dead body.

Chapter 88

Whit

UNFORTUNATELY, THE CHARGING TRAIN didn't stop at the abandoned station we'd just left in the dust. The race was still on. The scraping, screeching sound of metal on metal made my jawbone rattle, but I continued to stomp on the gas pedal as hard as I could, the track's cross timbers making the van jolt unbearably.

It was starting to dawn on me that we'd never be able to outrun that train. In a few seconds, it would slam into us, probably spinning us sideways, then smashing us flat against the tunnel's cement wall.

I need another tunnel, I thought. *I need a turnoff.*

Problem was, I had no idea how to create one magically, and Wisty was busy being a mouse. I couldn't think straight. Every bit of energy I had was focused on just holding on to the jouncing, jerking steering wheel and pressing the gas pedal almost through the floor.

"There!" Emmet shouted, pointing. "There! Whit, look!"

I saw it—a turnoff. The track actually split into two up ahead.

"Which way?" I yelled. "We don't know which one the train will take!"

Emmet's face was bone white as he stared wildly at the fork. I knew he had no way of knowing any more than I did. The train's whistle continued to blare, as if the driver thought it would make us come to our senses and get the heck out of his way.

"Okay!" I yelled over the crazy din. "Okay! I think I know what to do!"

We sped toward the split, the train's light filling our van like those overexposed scenes on TV where somebody always dies. I jerked into the right-hand tunnel, then flicked my left hand in back of me.

In my mind, I saw the track switch moving just as we passed over it.

The barreling train suddenly swerved and plunged into the left-hand tunnel, shooting away from us like a comet. Within seconds its terrifying whistle had faded to a dull whine.

We finally bounced to a stop, but I kept the engine running, just in case. My shirt was stuck to me with cold sweat.

The kids sobbed and hugged one another in the backseat. Emmet was still white as an alabaster statue and looked like he was going to either cry with relief or barf from motion sickness. Margo's tense hands gripped the dashboard like claws, and then she reached over and grabbed my shoulder just as hard.

"You did it, Whit," she whispered. "You saved our lives."

It took us a few minutes to catch our breath and come down from the adrenaline-cliff edge. Then Emmet's voice hissed excitedly through the sounds of celebration.

"*This* is the, uh, turnoff I was telling you about." His voice was still shaking. "We can take the tunnel to the portal. And, from there, we'll return safely to the basement of Garfunkel's." He leaned back in his seat, shell-shocked.

A tiny voice came from the rear of the van. "Are we really going to Garfunkel's?"

Chapter 89

Wisty

I SCREAMED AND LET GO OF THE ROPE, landing painfully on the concrete. As the wind crept back into my lungs, I rolled over to look up at the swollen corpse.

There was a sign pinned to his chest—written in the large font of New Order officialdom—that read:

FAILURE TO EXECUTE NEW ORDER ORDERS
NECESSITATES THE EXECUTION OF HE WHO FAILED!

They had killed the Visitor for our escape.

I was almost starting to feel bad for him when a half-dozen enormous hands grabbed me. Roughly. The crew-cut, neckless bruisers hoisted me into the air and threw me against the concrete wall.

The leader jabbed a massive finger into my face and literally sprayed his rage at me. "Nobody. Ever. ESCAPES!" he screamed.

Something was broken inside of me. Feisty girl Wisty would have fought. Truant Wisty would have said something sarcastic back—like pointing out that I had actually been breaking *into* this place rather than busting *out*. Bad, scary witch Wisty would have thrown a lightning bolt to teach him a good lesson about bullying girls who were one-quarter his size.

But my magic was dead.

I don't know how to describe it, but it was like that little spark was gone.

So what did I do? Why, I burst into tears, of course.

Predictably enough, they mocked me. "Aw, the poor little thing," one snickered, and another inanely quipped, "Well, one thing's clear—with that many tears, I guess we've been giving her too much water."

Which gave me the brilliant idea to spit in the guy's face. In the absence of magic, there's always saliva.

Okay, so it wasn't one of my best ideas.

"Aaargh!" he screamed and grabbed my hair, twisting my head backward so hard I could almost see the tips of my toes dragging on the floor behind me. It felt like my neck might break.

This is the part where I'm supposed to explode into flame.

But there was no magic. Nothing.

Nothing.

Nothing.

Chapter 90

Wisty

"I DON'T UNDERSTAND IT. We aren't missing any prisoners from the cell blocks," the administrator told my guards. He was a neat little man who carried himself stiffly, probably trying to make sure he didn't seem a fraction of an inch shorter than he was. "We had three transferred to the infirmary after interrogation last night, but every other inmate is present and accounted for."

I felt the blood drain completely from my face. They'd injured three kids in interrogation?! At this point, it shouldn't have surprised me that this cruel New Order would *torture,* but still, my despair sank to a new low.

"I'm going to ask you again," he said, turning to me. "What's your cell block?"

I was so torn apart I couldn't even respond. He thought I was being defiant. But I knew the sad truth: I didn't have much defiance left in me anymore.

The administrator's headset glowed blue, and he turned away. He was getting a call.

"No, her hair hasn't been cut to specifications. Yes, it *is* red..." Suddenly his face flushed, and he stood even more erect as he turned to regard me.

"Yes," he continued, "about five feet two and not much more than a hundred pounds, I'd say.... Yes, yes." His face broke into a prideful smile. "It certainly *is* a piece of good fortune."

And then he said the words that really rocked my world.

"Now we only have to find her brother and parents, and the Allgood threat will be history."

"What?!" I yelled.

The guards shoved me painfully back against the wall for daring to interrupt his conversation.

"Yes... very good," he went on. "Consider it done... and congratulations to *you* too." The administrator's headset switched off, and he smiled at me mockingly.

"My parents aren't in this prison?!" I shrieked at him, earning myself another bruising shove from the guards.

"Why would we put your parents in a children's prison?" He snorted.

"I don't know," I said. "Because you're all certifiably insane?"

The guards gave me yet another jab, but the administrator ignored me. "Why, indeed, would we keep them alive at all? *You,* we need to interrogate, but them... trust me, as soon as we have them, you can officially call yourself an orphan."

He smiled menacingly, but for all his cruelty, I was taking some comfort in the fact that my parents were alive... and *free*.

"Put her in cell block D, cell four twelve," he yelled at the guards, who dragged me away from his post and toward the place where I would spend the rest of my short life.

I stared around at the cell doors, their bars crowded with the hollow-eyed faces of kids, none over the age of sixteen.

A new anger was building inside me. Was Sasha a New Order spy? Had he fooled Whit and me to come here just so we'd be captured?

They dragged me up the stairs and over to cell 412, which, like all of them, was crowded with haunted, hopeless faces. How much longer would they be alive? How much longer would *any* of us be alive?

Chapter 91

Wisty

ONE THOUGHT HAUNTED ME as the guards shoved me against the bars and went to open the door. Even if Sasha had tricked us, the fact was that I'd *failed*. I'd failed these kids. I'd failed Emmet. I'd failed Margo. I'd failed Whit. I'd failed my parents.

For the second time that day, I cried like a baby.

But then the most remarkable thing happened. One of the kids, an emaciated little girl inside the cell, touched my arm through the bars and tried to cheer me up.

"Don't cry. Remember, they're doing all this because they're scared. They're afraid of you. They're afraid of all of us."

"What do you mean?"

"They know we can change everything. They know we have the power to fight back."

"Shut up, you little piece of dirt!" one guard barked at her like a hellhound. The girl didn't even flinch.

Which got me thinking. Here she was, emaciated and oppressed to the brink of death—a veritable Michael Clancy—and yet she had the strength to comfort me. She had the strength to hope.

Maybe I had just a flicker of faith inside me too. That 1 percent chance of survival that I'd hung on to so fiercely earlier.

They're afraid of you. They're afraid of all of us.

I turned to my hellhound guards as they manhandled me toward the now open cell door and heard myself yell like a girl possessed, "FREEZE!"

They laughed, and one of them clouted me over the head with a nightstick.

Stars danced in my vision, and I went limp. What was going on? I couldn't hear the guards....I was no longer being dragged....And the kids in the cell were staring openmouthed like they'd just seen Santa Claus come down the chimney.

Yes. *Yes!* Some magic had worked! The guards were frozen!

With some minor straining of my wrists and elbows, I managed to pry myself loose of their stonelike grip.

It was still a long, long way to freedom. I stared up at the winking red light of a security camera that was even now swiveling toward me. Who knew how many hundreds of guards and dozens of steel doors I was going to have to get past to reach the outside?

And not just me, but my big fat conscience too. After

all, the kids in my open cell could come with me, but what about all the hundreds of other haunted, pitiful faces looking at me in wonder through the bars of nearby cells? And the ones on the next level? And in the next cell block?

I took the master key from the belt of one of the frozen guards and moved down to the adjacent cell.

"You guys want to get out of here or what?" I yelled down the cell block.

My question was rewarded with hundreds of heartbreakingly hopeful cheers. I quickly made my way along the balcony, unlocking each cell as I went.

Then a siren began to wail, and about twenty guards stormed into the cell block.

Chapter 92

Wisty

THE JACKBOOTED BULLIES forged into the crowd of children I'd released from their cells, swinging clubs and firing stun guns with unfathomable cruelty.

The sight of two-hundred-pound-plus guards manhandling, beating, and hurting children, some of them a quarter their size, is something I will have nightmares about for the rest of my life.

At the time, it sickened me almost past the point of outrage. Every cell in my body seemed to boil with anger. And then... *whoosh!*

And I mean, *WHOOSH!* Familiar two-, three-, and four-feet flames once again swirled around me.

The Flame Girl Strikes Back.

Still, it wouldn't have made a lick of difference had I not had a massive stroke of luck right then.

The lucky strike was that I was right under a smoke alarm. And, time was, the people in charge of the world actually put a value on human life and put in a safety pre-caution so that not everybody in the prison would die in a massive fire. The New Order, in taking over a jail that had been created by a society based on fairness and justice, had neglected to realize that the fire alarms in the prison automatically opened all the interior doors, including the doors to the cells themselves.

And so, as the smoke alarm added its siren wail to the cacophony all around us, I charged the guards, leaving fiery footprints everywhere I stepped. I had to lead these kids out of here, and that meant I had to clear a path.

The guards didn't put up much resistance. I charged down the hallway after them all the way to the next cell block before they met reinforcements and tried to stand their ground. One guard was shouting orders into a walkie-talkie; the others had stun guns and nightsticks at the ready.

I took a deep breath and remembered what the kid had said: *They're afraid of all of us.*

Well, they clearly were at least a little afraid of a furi-ous fifteen-year-old firebrand flying toward them with her arms spread wide, screeching like a total maniac, *"Fire really, really hurts!"* and *"I'm a bad, scary witch!"*

I burst right through their ranks, not even a little upset by the shouting as their clothes caught on fire. Yelling *"Stop, drop, and roll, you idiots,"* I dashed into the next cell block.

"Everybody *out!"* I screamed at the kids there as well

as those from the last block, who had been following me—sensibly—at a safe distance. "Fire! Everyone get out. Right now! See that stairwell there? *That's the way out!*"

I was actually starting to feel a little scared myself. This was the longest I'd ever stayed on fire. Was there a point of no return from being charbroiled?

I couldn't think about it now, because suddenly hundreds of skinny, dirty, terrified kids were pouring past me. And them, I didn't want to catch on fire.

Chapter 93

Whit

AFTER WE DROPPED the kids off at Garfunkel's, we decided to bypass Death by Subway and take a different route back to the prison. True to my word, I avoided directions from Emmet at all costs.

This time Margo was my copilot. We were in the van alone; the others would meet us close to the prison gates.

I'd done a pretty successful "abracadabra" on the van before we left, turning it an uneven shade of dark blue, with Idaho license plates.

But that wasn't the only big change.

A short time ago I'd looked like I was about thirty years old. Then I'd changed back to a teenager—*with no warning*—right as I was going up the stalled escalator at Garfunkel's. It had made me trip and fall down several steps. Very uncool.

As Margo and I headed back to the prison, I thought

about that and wondered, *Has Wisty suddenly changed back into herself also? Has the spell simply worn out?*

I had no idea where she was, what she was doing, or what form she'd be in when I found her. Flat as a pancake, maybe? Or with one or two limbs, the rest left behind in a spring-action mousetrap?

"You look worried, Whit," Margo said with a concerned glance my way.

"Well, *yeah*," I said, in more of a "no duh" kind of voice than I'd intended. "Aren't you?"

"Yes and no," Margo said, surprising me. "I mean, sure, anything could happen. But... I mean, this is my life now. It's what I do. No parents, no brothers or sisters left. I have nothing to lose, really. And I have everything to gain by helping these kids and your mom and dad."

I sat in stunned silence. Then I said, "I'm sorry." I actually couldn't remember the last time I'd uttered those words with any real meaning. And I wasn't exactly sure why I said them now. But it felt right.

"Don't be *sorry*, Whit! I'm no big hero." Margo scoffed. "It's heroic to face your own pain, and you're the one who's facing that right now. I get it. You have a sister you love in there. You have parents who were wanted, dead or alive, in there. The love of your life is dead but still haunting you. Oh yeah, and I hear you're due to be executed on your birthday."

"Well, actually," I said with a weak smile, "they revised the order to execute me immediately."

"So when is your birthday, anyway?" she asked.

Wow. I really wasn't sure. Time had felt warped. And with all the portals we'd traveled through, time actually *was* warped.

I looked at Margo in surprise.

"I think it already happened."

"Well, how about that?" Margo said with a rare smile. "And you didn't even get to celebrate."

She continued to grin, her brown eyes shining brightly, and sucked in a deep breath. I knew a windup to a song when I saw one.

"Don't you dare—," I protested, but she went on gleefully.

"Happy birthday to you! Happy birthday to you! Happy birthday, dear Whit..."

She trailed off as her gaze shifted past me, and then she frowned. "What's *that?* There, in the top windows of the main building?"

I jerked the van to a sudden stop. "It's flames. The prison is on fire."

Oh, Wisty, what have you done?

Chapter 94

Wisty

"GET OUT!" I shouted. "Get out of here now! *Fire!*"

The kids pattered barefoot down the metal stairs, most of them unable to take their eyes off me. One of them finally squeaked, "But the guards—"

"Forget the guards!" I screamed with a new level of hysteria I didn't know I had in me. "The guards are afraid of you. They're afraid of me. *They're afraid of everything!*"

A new burst of energy surged through the kids. As soon as the first one reached the ground floor, I pointed toward the main doors, careful not to get too close to any of them.

More New Order guards began arriving now, billy clubs out, but I rushed straight at them, arms open. They drew back as if I were the plague. "Stay where you are!" I warned them. "You come near me, and I won't give you a choice between regular and extracrispy!"

By now waves of kid prisoners were pushing through

the main exit, escaping right underneath a huge portrait of The One Who Is The One. It occurred to me that I didn't even know if Whit and the others were waiting outside.

"Out, out!" I shouted, my voice hoarse now. I was starting to feel a little hot and crackly, and I hoped I wasn't cooked extracrispy myself.

Flames started to lick around the office doorway, and then the whole room was ablaze. I'd left a stream of several fires in my wake. With any luck, after the kids got out, this hideous prison would burn to the ground.

It seemed to take forever for the last kids to get through the hallway and out the doors as the guards avoided the flames in terror or tried to extinguish their own personal infernos. Meanwhile, I was getting so hot that it didn't seem out of the realm of possibility that I might explode like a piece of popcorn in a microwave.

By the time the last prisoner passed out the gate, the few guards who were left were ready for vengeance. They lumbered toward me, zombielike and charred, waving their billy clubs.

"Uh-uh!" I warned them. "Or I'll burn you to cinders!"

Then I turned tail and raced out the exit myself, touching the walls and anything else I could reach as I went by. Streaks and handprints of fire marked my path. Cool — I mean, *hot!*

Then finally I saw streaks of moonlight, and the outer doors ahead of me, and then, at last, the final gates.

Please be there, Whit, I prayed. *Please, wizard.*

The inner courtyard was filling rapidly with more guards and New Order soldiers. But then I heard Feffer barking like the hellhound she'd been trained to be. I could see her scaring the bejesus out of some guards as Margo herded kids outside to safety.

I did a fast head count. Margo, Feffer, Emmet, Sasha... and yes, *Whit!* They were all there, helping the prisoners get away.

I was gasping for air, feeling completely burned out, like there was nothing left of me for the fire to consume. Whit was looking all around, searching for me. *Am I so unrecognizable?*

Then he saw me, and alarm flashed in his eyes. Fear—like I'd never seen on his face before, not even the time he fell out of our tree and broke his leg in two places.

I tried to run to him, but the last thing I remember was falling to my knees and hearing a most hateful voice.

"Wisteria Allgood, you are condemned to death!" it said.

Chapter 95

Whit

I GAGGED AND CHOKED ON the smell of smoke and burning paint as more and more kids, hundreds of them, flowed out the doors of the Overworld Prison. It was a beautiful sight, really.

Bless Wisty, I thought. *She did it.* Now I just had to make sure she was safe and had found our mom and dad. Where was she? Where were they?

It had seemed like forever since we'd first caught sight of the flames in the prison windows, but it had just been minutes. "Hurry!" Margo was shouting as we herded more kids through the gates in a kind of fireman's line. "We've set up an escape route through the sewers!" Margo yelled.

I craned my neck, looking desperately for Wisty—as girl or mouse—but couldn't see her anywhere.

Was she with our folks? Or was my sister trapped inside the burning building? Had she been caught?

The street outside was filled with kids who were gathered

up by our second team, led by Sasha. Traffic had stopped, unable to move. Alarms everywhere were flashing and wailing. But still no Wisty.

Then the last kids burst through the doors, and I finally saw her — totally aflame.

It was different this time, worse — she was glowing more brightly, more white-hot than I had seen before. And her wild-eyed face, her newly gaunt frame, looked weaker, closer to terror and death than I ever could have imagined.

She saw me, and her face — even through the flames — sparkled with hope. But then her eyes rolled back in her head, and she dropped to the pavement like she'd been shot.

"Get the van!" I shouted over my shoulder to Margo as I made a break toward Wisty. "I'll bring Wisty!"

"I don't think so, wizard," came a terrible, gravelly voice right behind me.

Chapter 96

Whit

IT WAS LIKE a recurring nightmare of the worst kind.

There loomed the foul Matron, swaddled in bandages and pale as chalk. Next to her was The One Who Judges, Ezekiel Unger—her *brother,* I remembered—still in his depressing black robes, looking like the Grim Reaper.

Security "specialists" armed with scatterguns backed them up.

Next to them stood...our Jonathan. Looking smug and complicit.

Despair descended on me like a funeral shroud. It had never occurred to me that anyone from Freeland could stoop to the traitorous level of Byron Swain, but apparently Jonathan had.

"Jon?" Margo gasped.

Jonathan just shrugged. "It's too hard, and hopeless, living like you do. The New Order offers a better life," he said. "It beats prison and death. I believe in The One."

Margo's eyes filled with angry tears. She'd made me feel stronger before, and I wanted to make her believe that everything was going to be okay. Even if it really wasn't.

Words sprang into my brain. I didn't know where they came from. "Margo, they're afraid of us. They're afraid of everything." And then I kept on talking without really thinking, until it turned into a chant:

They're afraid of change, and we must change.
    They're afraid of the young, and we are the young.
They're afraid of music, and music is our life.
    They're afraid of books, and knowledge, and ideas.
They're most afraid of our magic.

Margo stared at me and sniffled, her eyes wide, but the tears were gone.

I scooped up Wisty—who was unconscious and nearly weightless in my arms—and said the words again. Louder and more forcefully this time.

They're afraid of us, they're afraid of everything.
    They're afraid of change, and we must change.
They're afraid of the young, and we are the young.

"*Silence!*" roared Judge Unger, his pinched beetle's face turning a shade of funereal purple.

"Wait till I get my hands on you again," the Matron

snarled at his side, her icy eyes narrowing into thin slits that wouldn't take a dime.

"I don't think so, Matron. Not going to happen," I said. "Actually, you are petrified of us. And you should be. We have the magic. You don't."

The next time I spoke the words, everyone—Margo, Emmet, Janine, the prison kids, everyone but Jonathan—-repeated them with me.

They're afraid of us, they're afraid of everything.
They're afraid of change, and we must change.
They're afraid of the young, and we are the young.
They're afraid of—

"*Enough!* More than enough, actually!" Judge Unger pounded his fist into his hand, then raised it as if he would hit me. "*The witch and wizard must be put to death at once!*"

In my arms, my sister suddenly opened her eyes. I stared at her in amazement.

Wisty's eyes had been blue before. Now they looked almost clear, like sea glass. Her hair was more auburn than its former red, more like our mother's. Her eyes glowed, and she tried her best to smile at me. "Hey, brother."

"You and your sister are going to burn. Right here in this prison!" Judge Unger spewed powerful hatred our way. "The fire's going to take care of our society's problem once and for all!

"You!" he snapped at the security specialists. "Take them back into the prison and lock all the doors! They like fire. Let them burn. That is my final judgment. It is the law of the land. I am The One Who Judges!"

"*No!*" came a powerful voice.

Wisty's voice.

Chapter 97

Whit

"I DON'T THINK SO," Wisty went on as she unwrapped herself from my arms. I had no idea what she was up to, but I knew I couldn't stop her. She turned her head slowly to look at the Matron, then stared at Judge Unger. I sensed a spell coming on, and I cringed involuntarily. We didn't have time for trial and error.

"Trust me," Wisty whispered to me. She turned back to our accusers. "You say that you're The One," she said with a tone of authority I'd never heard in her before. "But your form will now *become undone*."

For the first time in all of Wisty's spellcasting, a shiver went through me.

"We're a witch and wizard," Wisty continued, her voice sounding stronger and stronger.

As you can clearly tell.
  But since you don't deserve

Where you presently dwell,
  It is now with great pleasure
We send you off to—

We all waited with bated breath…and fear, I must admit, and trembling. I almost didn't want to hear her complete the curse.

"Um, *Roachland*," Wisty finished. "Where you will be judged a heinous criminal even under the laws of roaches!"

She snapped her hands at Judge Unger, who actually cowered.

"I give you all my power," I whispered to my sister. "You speak for both of us."

It was as if lightning were moving within me, a feeling of quicksilver warmth that raced through my hands and into Wisty.

Again, she snapped her hands at Judge Unger. This time, he shrieked, and a crackling burst of white light surrounded him, engulfing the monster from his head to the tips of his black riding boots.

We all waited, hearts in our throats, and then, when the smoke cleared, the biggest, ugliest roach I'd ever seen lay trembling on the pavement.

The Matron stared at the hideous creature, appalled.

"You're next," Wisty told her.

The Matron shot a glance at the security specialists, and they shook their heads. Whirling, they ran through the crowd as fast as they could. Jonathan too.

The last I saw of the Matron, she was lumbering away, shrieking like a banshee. She had gotten our message; now she would help spread it—right up to the Council of Ones. *The fight is on!*

Wisty's eyes grew very large. "I think...we did it!" she said, her voice raspy and weak. Her eyes were turning back to blue again.

"Eww!" I heard a kid squeal. I looked down to see a large rat darting through everyone's legs. Suddenly, it seized the roach—and bit off its head.

It struck me as being one of the top five grossest things I'd ever seen, but Wisty was having a laugh attack.

"What's so funny?" I asked her.

"Now that's justice!" she said as the rat skittered away with the rest of Ezekiel Unger's roach body in its mouth.

"You know," she continued, "I like rats *much* better when they're not bigger than me. They're almost cute, don't you think?"

And then she fainted again.

Yeah, my sister's weird.

Mostly in a good way.

Chapter 98

Whit

NOW HERE'S WHAT my sister missed: I turned and saw that several of the prison kids were crying, bawling their little eyes out, shivering, cowering.

The One Who Is The One had appeared—this time with no strong winds, no warning of any kind.

He stood directly over Wisty and declared, "She's good. She's *very good*, Whitford. You both are. Of course, you must know that I had no intention of letting either of you be seriously harmed. No, no, no."

I finally found my voice. "I'll bet you didn't."

"I absolutely didn't. That isn't one of the prophecies. Even I can't change those."

The One looked hard at me then, almost stared right through me. "You do know the prophecies about you and your sister, don't you? That's what all the fuss is about. Your parents didn't tell you? You mean, *no one* has? *You don't know?*"

I wished I could hurt him, but all I could do was dumbly mutter, "What prophecies?"

"Oh Whit, Whit, poor Whit.... All right then, I'll have to be the bearer of legend and myth. Listen well.

"*Prophecy One: a boy and girl, brother and sister, shall be born to Wiccans and shall achieve powers heretofore unrealized by any other Wiccans.* That much is obviously true.

"*Prophecy Two: the boy and girl shall lead an army of children to victory....* Well, look around. You won the Battle of the New Order Reformatory, didn't you?

"*Three: the brother and sister shall know great sadness, suffering, and terrible betrayal.* Hope not. Think so.

"*Four: they must visit all five Levels of Reality, which no one before them has done, and learn the lessons of each level.* Sounds even worse than middle school and high school.

"*Prophecy Five:* well, I'll come back to that one.

"*Six: ultimately, the brother and sister shall combine with an even greater power for the goodness and prosperity of all.* Sounds exciting, no?"

The One stared deeply into my eyes, and it was almost as if he were trying to know me better, to understand something about me.

"So, Whitford, what do you think of all this? Am I friend or foe — or a little of each? Are the important things in life black and white, or maybe a little gray? Do fairies, elves, and gremlins exist? And will you ever see Celia again? I leave you with those weighty thoughts and questions.

"And this one last prophecy, sweet prince: *the Allgoods shall be executed*. That is Prophecy Five. I'm sure that you and your sister will sort it all out. Give her my very best. Wake her gently."

Chapter 99

Wisty

"WHAT HAPPENED?" I asked dreamily when I opened my eyes and caught sight of Whit.

"You just had a bad dream, Wisty. You've been sick for days. Mom and Dad and I have been really worried about you."

This is what I *hoped* to hear, anyway.

Then I caught sight of Margo, Sasha, and Emmet in the background. There was a moment of letdown, sure, but then I felt huge relief, knowing they were okay and they were there for me. Even that hateful weasel, Byron Swain, actually seemed concerned about me.

"Don't you remember?" Whit said. "The prison, Judge Unger, the Matron, all the kids who escaped?"

"I do!" I said, trying to sit up. "Actually, I do. Most of it anyway."

"You missed The One Who Is The One," Whit said then.

"I did? How? When?"

"I'll tell you later. What about Mom and Dad?" Whit asked suddenly, his face lit with concern when he saw mine fall. "What happened? Where are they? Wisty? What's wrong?"

My eyes went from face to face until they came to Sasha's. "Ask *him*," I said. "He's the one who lied to us. Mom and Dad were never in the prison. Sasha lied to get us to help." Bitterness rose in my throat. "I'll never forgive you!" I spat out.

It took a moment for Whit to process the betrayal. In a flash his expression morphed from disbelief to dismay to disgust.

"No," Whit growled, his fists clenched. "Neither will I!"

Sasha never flinched. "Worse things have happened to me. Far worse. We needed you guys. This is a war against true evil. The ends justify any effective means." Then Sasha gave us that cheery smile of his, and it was so, so sad. And creepy.

Then and there, I vowed never to let the "war" or anything else do that to me. "I should turn you into a slug!" I shouted at Sasha. "You used our friendship, and ruined it forever."

"Take it easy!" Whit cautioned. "You've been out for hours. He's not worth it."

"She's awake!" someone shouted, and I suddenly realized that all around me were hundreds of kids wearing, like, party hats and blowing noisemakers. Tattered paper streamers were draped everywhere. We were back at Garfunkel's.

Feffer was sitting on a couch, eating what looked like cake off a paper plate. When she heard my voice, she jumped off and came to me, licking my face.

I got to my feet, shaky, starving, and a little light-headed. Janine, our leader of the week, pushed through the crowd, holding a soda and a plate of chocolate cake. *Real cake!* Totally pukka. I hadn't had any in . . . it felt like a lifetime. I didn't even use a fork. I dug into it, icing first.

"To the Liberators!" Janine shouted. Everyone around me echoed her words.

My face flushed as I tried to smile and shove more cake into my mouth at the same time.

"Everyone helped," Whit said. "Here's to all of you!"

Margo, the commando, was staring at Whit, who did look very heroic. "You two did the most."

"So, for today, enjoy being heroes!" Janine said, but her eyes shone only on Whit. I knew he didn't notice that she was totally crushing on him. My bro was clueless, as usual. That's one thing I love about him.

Someone handed me a foot-long hot dog with every-thing slopped all over it, and I began to wolf down the frank right on top of the cake. Yuck, but also delish.

"Emphasis being on 'today,'" Emmet clarified with a heart-stopping grin. "We don't let anybody be heroes for more than one day, because it goes to their heads. Hero worship tends to corrupt. Or at least turn you into an erlenmeyer."

"Understood," said Whit.

"However," Janine went on, "for going above and beyond the call of duty, you are hereby promoted to official rescue mission driver. We stashed the van in a secret hideout behind enemy lines, and it's waiting for you next time we go raiding."

"*That* death trap?" Whit said.

"That *rescue vehicle*," said Janine. "We just heard from another group of kids in an abandoned mall. They need help badly."

"Wha—?" I blurted, my mouth still full.

"They need help," Janine repeated, as if that explained all of life's complex mysteries...and maybe it did.

"Another mission?" Whit said, but I could see the gears in his mind turning. His eyes met mine, and I could tell we were both thinking the same thing: our parents were out there too.

"Well, okay," I said finally, and Whit nodded.

Feffer nudged my leg, and I patted her. "Of course you're going," I assured her.

"And me," said a voice up close to my ear.

Chapter 100

Wisty

I TURNED TO SEE Byron Traitor Suck-up Weasel perched on a shelf near my head, curled into a snaky little S.

"No. You are *not* going," I said firmly. "You are not going anywhere with us. You are still a hateful, traitorous, black-hearted *naysayer!*"

"Nuh-uh," said Byron, in a tone that I think confirmed my point. Someone had given him half a hot dog, and he was chomping through it. "I've changed. I like you guys now. I want to go with you."

"You are so full of it," I said. "You're staying right here."

In my peripheral vision I caught Janine, Margo, and Emmet violently shaking their heads.

"He has to go with you," Janine said. "You brought him. He's your responsibility. The weasel *must go.*"

"There's something I want to say to you guys," Byron said stiffly. "I want to apologize." My eyes widened. "At the time, when we...*met,* I felt I was doing the right thing. It seemed to be the only smart thing to do, to act like I did. But after seeing the kids living in Freeland, and the Hospital where you guys were, and the Curve dog…and realizing about how maybe I could have done something different in terms of that whole thing with my sister…well…I'm just saying I feel *differently*," he continued. "That's all I wanted to say."

Whit and I made surprised faces at each other.

"Fine," Whit said, and sighed. "Fine. We'll take him along."

And then another strange thing: tears, actual tears, began to flow from the hateful weasel's eyes.

Can people really change? I wondered. *Maybe they can.*

EPILOGUE

THERE'S NO PLACE LIKE HOME

Chapter 101

Wisty

IT WAS MORE THAN a little scary to be on our own, me and Whit, in a stolen van. Well, that was the deal—just us, except for our budding pet shop: Feffer and Byron, the World's Most Annoying Pointy-Headed Formerly Traitorous Weasel.

With our clean clothes and tidied hair—my beautiful *auburn* hair—we sure looked like New Order kids, so we would probably be safer. We were learning to rely on our magic more and trust in our powers. It's harder than you would think.

Whit had been telling me about seeing his Oneness again, and hearing the prophecies about us, which didn't include the one we saw on the wall inside Garfunkel's. Also, poor Whit was seriously pining for Celia, hoping for a dream visit, at least. As for me, I was just enjoying the ride, blasting Stonesmack's first album with the van's stereo speakers turned up. Way up.

"Here. Need some help," said Byron, bringing me the

end of a large bandanna. "If you tie this to the clothes-hanger thingy, I'll have a nice little hammock."

I took the bandanna and turned around in my seat. He'd already somehow fastened one end to a handhold. Resigned, I slung the other end over the small clothes-hanger hook next to me, then tied a knot for him.

"That's what I'm talkin' about!" Byron jumped up and curled himself into his little hammock, leaving only his pointy face showing.

I sighed.

"Hey," said Whit, "this looks familiar, doesn't it? Check it out."

I scanned the landscape through my window. We'd been passing fields of crops, mostly corn, with signs saying CLEAN CORN FOR CLEAN PEOPLE: WE GUARANTEE THIS PRODUCT HAS NOT BEEN SPRAYED, GENETICALLY MODIFIED, OR TAMPERED WITH BY SPELLCASTERS. BROUGHT TO YOU BY THE NEW ORDER COUNCIL OF AGRICULTURE.

Weird stuff like that, probably written by The One Who Makes Irritating Billboards.

I saw what Whit meant, though. Something about the shape of the land, the way the horizon looked—it was familiar to me too. My back and neck tensed. Familiarity breeds, I don't know, *paranoia?*

"What's that?" asked Whit, pulling the van over to the side of the highway and pointing toward a shape in the distance, something poking up out of the unending sea of orderly crops.

"A tree?" I said, and had the most horrible feeling settle in my stomach. Why would the N.O. have left a single tree standing?

We climbed out of the van and, without a word to each other, began walking toward it, Feffer in tow. We crossed a few fields and some paths that, underneath a layer of dust, we could tell were abandoned streets, with double-yellow lines down the middle.

It took us half an hour or so to walk to it, and all the while the pit of my stomach dropped farther and farther.

But I didn't truly feel like I was going to throw up until I saw the birdhouse.

Our birdhouse. The birdhouse Dad had built for Whit and me, and our mom. Nailed just where it had always been, twenty feet up on the massive trunk of the oak tree in our backyard.

How many times had I looked up at that spreading oak tree? My dad said it had been there for a hundred years or more. Whit and I had climbed it when we were little. Whit had used its acorns for batting practice, plinking them sometimes all the way over the neighbor's roof. Also, he had fallen from that tree, breaking his leg like it was made of peanut brittle.

Now the tree stood by itself at the edge of a recently planted New Order field.

Everything around it, every house—ours included—was gone.

Chapter 102

Wisty

"WHERE'S OUR HOUSE? Where are Mom and Dad?" I said in a whisper, looking at the rippling corn patch where we used to live, where we had grown up, where we'd had such unbelievably happy times — except maybe my school-detention days.

I remembered what Mom had said whenever we came back from a vacation. I remembered every word.

North, east, south, and west
Our home is in the center.
Though we may roam, our home is best
And speak love, you may enter.

To be honest, I'd never really understood it, and the last line had never made any sense. Speak *of* love? Speak *about* love? Someone's nickname *is* Love, and she's telling him to speak?

I murmured the rhyme again, as mystified by it as I had been by everything else that'd happened since my normal life became my nightmare life.

"And speak love, you may enter," Whit mused.

"Speak love," I repeated, my heart aching. Then … "Oh. Wait. Speak love!"

I stepped forward, closer to where our front steps had been.

"Love," I said loudly and clearly. *"Love."*

Then I held my breath as a ghostly shape began to form in front of us. It was our home, vaporous, see-through, not totally real. But the memory of our house, the essence of our house, was here, right down to the ivy that climbed the southern wall and an old deflated football of Whit's.

Then the front door opened, and I felt my heart thudding heavily inside my chest.

Please. Not The One, I prayed.

Chapter 103

Wisty

"MOM," I WHISPERED as her form started down the steps. "Dad."

They came to us, and of course we wanted to hug them, but we couldn't, any more than Whit could hug Celia.

A horrible realization dawned on me. "Are you Half-lights?" I asked, my voice twisting hideously, on the verge of a bawl. "Are you *dead?*"

"We're not dead, Wisty," Mom said. "We're just some-place else. You'll see the real us soon enough. I hope so."

"Mom," I said again, my jubilation at her words almost making me faint. Could my emotions possibly roller-coaster any worse than this? I threw my arms out and tried to hug her again.

"Why can't we touch you, then?"

"My sweet darlings," Mom said, and it was pure *her.* "We're alive, trust me. But we're not really here right now. Magic has brought us to you today....Someone else's magic."

Dad chimed in. "The important thing is that you know we're so very proud of you. Your time in prison. How you rescued the children. How you dealt with that evil and unworthy judge. And The One Who Thinks He Is The One. You've done amazingly well."

"You two are the present, and the future," Mom said, smiling. "And now we know you can do it. This has just been a warm-up."

"A warm-up...for what?" I asked. "I just want to be home again."

Mom smiled wistfully. "You'll see. But first you have to believe, Wisty, that you're a very, very good witch. And one day, you'll be a famous musician too."

"And you're a very, very good wizard, Whit," Dad told him. "And, believe it or not, you're going to be an important writer."

Whit looked aghast. "I thought that the wizard thing was pretty out-there, Dad, but...a *writer*? You've got to be kidding."

"Do you have your journal?" Dad asked, still very serious, and then he looked at me. "And your drumstick? You haven't lost them, have you?"

I nodded and held up my drumstick. Whit pulled his journal out from his waistband. We'd gone to ridiculous lengths to keep these things safe, but for what reason? Because I was destined to be a musician? Because Whit — *Whit?* — was going to be an important writer? Who had time for writers and musicians in these dark days?

Mom held out a hand toward my beat-up, dirty drumstick. "Okay, Wisty, you've proven you're ready to do this. Transform that stick into its true form."

At this point, I was used to failing, but I *really* hated to fail in front of my parents. "Mom," I stalled, "you know I've got, like, a C-minus track record in that department."

"The difference is that now, I'm right here. You can look into my eyes. All of the secrets are in there."

When is the last time you really, really looked deep into your parents' eyes? I bet you don't even remember the last time. Like, maybe since you were a baby and making stupid googly eyes at each other. Well, you'd be surprised at what happens when you go in there. It's kind of scary, actually—but in a good way. I'm not going to tell you any more. Just try it yourself someday.

"Speak love, you may enter," Mom murmured. And I did.

And when I looked at the drumstick, it had turned into a dark, slender wand. You heard me. A witch's *magic wand*.

Like me, you probably thought a wand was just a fantastical figment of legends and fairy tales. Well, we were both wrong. For one of the few times in my life, I was speechless.

"Now, you do it, Whit. Open the journal and look at me." Dad held his hands above Whit's shoulders and, as Mom and I watched them speak wordlessly to each other, the journal filled in with lessons, explanations, magic spells—everything a witch and wizard would need to know.

Whit whispered to me, "I'm glad I didn't leave it in prison."

"We adore you both," Mom told us. "But we have to say good-bye for now."

"We love you," called Dad. "Good-bye. For a while anyway."

"No! *Stay!*" I cried, but Mom and Dad had already started to fade. "Mom! I love you! Come back! Please don't leave us already. Please!" I cried.

Then suddenly my parents were gone. Our house was gone too. Even the birdhouse.

I sank to my knees in the sun. Feffer licked my face. Dogs just know what to do, don't they?

Finally, I struggled to my feet, and Whit hugged me and hugged me.

"This book is amazing," he said, obviously trying to cheer me up. "Look—this is what I'm talking about."

He held the book open under my nose. I sniffled and looked at it. Actually, it *was* amazing.

How to De-weasel Someone, the page read in fancy letters. I frowned and read on: *If you've accidentally turned someone into a weasel, and you don't wish them to remain a weasel, first you must...*

I looked at him. "*Shred* that page, please, will you?"

"I dunno. The weasel might come in handy as a human at some point. You never know. Anyway," he said, tugging at my sleeve, "we've got things to do, kids to save, a New Order to crush . . . witch."

"Okay, wizard." I sighed and followed Whit back through the cornfields to our battered blue van.

I was ready for whatever came our way—at least I thought so. After all, I was a bad, scary witch. And Whit was a supercool wizard.

Then the weirdness continued—emerging out of the corn from the same way we had come, Byron Swain appeared, de-weaseled.

"Don't look at me like that," he said. "Your mom did it. She said I should watch over you two."

And off we went to crush the New Order.

Except things didn't go exactly according to plan.

Just according to the prophecies.

EPILOGUE
THE LAST...

Chapter 104

Wisty

WHICH, OF COURSE, brings us back to where we began: waiting to be hung until dead in a stadium filled past capacity with craven looky-loos, and presided over by a fiend in black robes who scares the snot out of me.

Seriously, The One Who Is The One radiates like he's some sort of bad-energy power plant.

And the most unnerving part isn't just the obvious power he has over the people in this stadium, from the officious security guards posted at every entrance to the slack-jawed gang of spectator teens in colorful N.O. sweatshirts sitting on the goalpost at the end of the field.

No, the thing that freaks me out is that I can tell he's got *magic*. A *lot* of it. Serious mojo.

His Oneness gestures for the crowd to quiet, and they hush even before his hand is fully raised. How often in human history has somebody like him taken control of a whole society? You know the answer, my friends: *far too often.*

It looks like he's going to give a speech, which will definitely put me over the edge. I mean, it's bad enough that his evil puss is going to be among the last things we Allgoods see, but now his words are going to be among the last things we hear.

That is, unless this vague but growing feeling I have is in fact some sort of witch's intuition. See, I have this weird sensation that at the last moment we're going to find a way out of this horrible, unspeakable situation...and live to fight on, and hopefully have something to do with bringing goodness and prosperity to all, aka Prophecy Six.

But that moment isn't here yet. In *this* moment, there's just quiet.

How can a hundred thousand people be so absolutely quiet?

So quiet you can hear the faint breeze riffling through the stadium.

So quiet there's nothing to do but be scared, really scared.

So, how are *you* doing—wherever you are? Listen, please: *seize the moment,* however worried you may be about what's coming next. It's your brain, it's your life, it's your attitude....Go out there and fill up with sights, sounds, and ideas that are bigger than yourself. We all know from history—to say nothing of this current reality—what can happen if we stay quiet and just do what's put in front of us.

And don't worry too much about Whit and me. Word of what happens next will get to you.

I promise.

And I'm a scary witch who keeps her promises.

TO BE CONTINUED

Excerpts of
NEW ORDER
PROPAGANDA

as Disseminated by
The Council of N.O. "Arts"

ESPECIALLY OFFENSIVE BOOKS THAT HAVE BEEN BANNED
as Dictated by The One Who Bans Books

THE BLUEPRINTS OF BRUNO GENET: A particularly repugnant, rule-breaking experiment in mixing dramatic text with pictures. This story of a young inventor distracted many readers—young and old alike—and greatly reduced measurable productivity at schools, workplaces, and residences around the world.

MARGARET'S PEN: The tale of a little girl, the barnyard animal she loves, and an unexpectedly small friend who saves the day. In the face of this ridiculous premise, its immense popularity is a prime example of just how flawed human society was in the days before the New Order.

THE PITCHER IN THE WHEAT: An immensely corruptive "coming-of-age" tale about a youth who endeavors to infect the populace with his cynicism and world-weariness.

THE THUNDER STEALER: This piece of fiction, steeped with references to some of the more outlandish legends of the Old World, is about a boy, Percival Johnson, who steals from the gods and brings down all kinds of divine wrath—and misadventure—upon himself. The entire series about this Percival Johnson is forbidden.

RATTERS' TRIP DOWN: The patently improbable saga of a pack of talking rodents who find their lives turned upside down by encroaching human development.

GARY BLOTTER AND THE GUILD OF REJECTS: The deeply troubling story of a delusional boy who realizes his job as a scribe is much easier when he uses his so-called magical powers.

THE FIREGIRL SAGA: This bizarre thread of folklore, which promotes secretive "love" relationships between humans and nonhumans, once bred massive, manic cults of creature-worshipping females.

THE ELDEST DRAGON: This epic fairy tale not only illogically suggests that persons under the age of twenty-one are suitable for leadership roles but is also offensive in its glorification of the long-proved-mythical fire-breathing lizard.

SOME PARTICULARLY REPREHENSIBLE NOISE POLLUTERS OF THE FORMER AGE
as Defined by The One Who Monitors Auditory Stimuli

The Groaning Bones: Their lineup changed over the many decades they made their so-called rock and roll, but—from horrible songs such as "Emerald Wednesday" to "[I've Got No] Retribution"—they were among the most successful bands of their benighted era.

Ron Sayer: This young blues-rock star somehow won awards, dated superstars, and wowed audiences with songs such as "Your Skin Is an Amusement Park."

B4: The band from Emerald Isle that took the world by storm in the original New Wave (which was a musical movement and altogether different from and in no way related to the New Order) and then took the world by storm again a decade later, and then the decade after that.... One of the most popular, and outspoken, bands of that deluded epoch.

We Shall Be Titans: A patently silly but nevertheless popular rock band that often featured the accordion, and whose deeply peculiar songs had been featured in the sound tracks of prime-time TV shows back in the days when there was more than One channel.

WWA: Wizards with Attitude, the seditious group that paved the lamentable road to hard-core wizard rap.

Stonesmack: Their album *A Flood of Redness to the Face* quickly catapulted this band to supergroup status, where they remained until Order came to the world.

The Walking Heads: They began as "art" rockers but ended up superstars. One of their filmed concerts documents just how insane their fans must have been to actually pay to see them.

Toasterface: An "alt-rock" band that was foolish enough to release an album for free to their fans, thus denying economic benefit to their era's tax collectors.

Lay-Z: A rapper whose biting, streetwise rap became so successful that he stopped bothering to finish his albums and lost touch with his fans.

311

MUSEUMS THAT HAVE THANKFULLY BEEN RAZED BY THE NEW ORDER

as Mandated by The One Who Micromanages Public Gathering Spaces

POPA: The Pavilion of Progressive Art. Located in the artistically unsound City of New Gotham, this glass-walled monstrosity was the repository for many of the most laughable pieces of art in what was considered—at the time—the great modern age.

The Britney: Also in the wicked City of New Gotham, this depraved institution became famous for its biennial exhibition of aesthetically questionable, morally reprehensible displays of garbage, which its patrons claimed to be the most current of "artistic expressions."

The Betelheim: This structurally unsound, spiral-shaped museum was one of the most bizarre gallery spaces in the former world.

The Jonesonian: The national museum of one of the largest and least-tasteful countries on earth. It was in fact comprised of submuseums covering everything from postage stamps to airplanes to sculpture.

The Fate Gallery: Incorporating one of the world's largest collections of both ancient and what was referred to as "modern" art, this museum is a prime example of why the last civilization came to an abrupt end.

The Fusili: Located in one of the older Old World cities, this was one of the most famous art museums of its time. It contained many pieces from an era that was referred to as the "Renaissance" but clearly was the height of the "Dark Ages."

VISUAL "ARTISTS" WHO ARE NO LONGER SULLYING THE WORLD

as Annotated by The One Who Assesses Visual Stimuli

Pepe Pompano: Considered by many the most significant painter in the former world's penultimate century. His "art" resembled the work of a kindergartner. One of his paintings, *Magia*—which apparently depicts a bombed-out city—was so large it took nearly twenty minutes to burn completely.

Wiccan Trollack: A bizarrely popular painter whose work involved exploding cans of paint.

Max Earnest: A deeply disturbed painter and sculptor who had no sense of proportion and whose works might have been hung in prisons to punish criminals—except that would have been grossly inhumane.

De Glooming: There is some debate about whether De Glooming was a real person or an elaborate hoax to prove just how poor the artistic tastes of his time were. The choice of shapes and color in De Glooming's art can only be described as nauseating.

Margie O'Greefle: During the Unfortunate Era, when females were not adequately controlled and monitored in their artistic expressions, this woman popularized flat, dull imagery completely devoid of detail and any representational accuracy.

Freida Halo: Another renegade female "artist" who frequently overindulged in uncomfortable, unseemly, unattractive self-portraits, also in the Unfortunate Era, when self-portraiture went unregulated. In these more enlightened, uncomplicated times, portraiture has been wisely limited to imagery of the Council of Ones.

EGREGIOUSLY INEFFICIENT OR SUBVERSIVE WORDS BANNED FROM USE
by Decree of The One Who Edits The Dictionary

<u>cantrip</u> (noun)
a. a magic trick or witch's spell b. chicanery <*usage instance:* Tabitha's slide into the dark arts began with *cantrips* and ended with life imprisonment.>

<u>curve</u> (noun)
a. the part of a line that bends b. in graphs, a line that indicates a quantity that increases *and* decreases at varying quantities against which it is measured c. *capitalized:* in myth and legend of the previous era, a person or animal capable of entering and traveling through a passageway to another universe or dimension of existence; cf. Straight and Narrow <*usage instance:* At the end of the folktale, a young *Curve* ended up in

another dimension, where he wandered the Fogroads of Hell until the end of time.>

Dickensian (adjective)
denoting poverty and distress of the type that occurred before The One Who Is The One saved the Overworld <*usage instance:* Until the New Order took over, 99 percent of the world's population existed in *Dickensian* straits.>

erlenmeyer (noun)
a person so insistent on scientific or rational explanation that he or she demonstrates social behavior generally deemed to be awkward <*usage instance:* The pitiless Resistance bullies taunted the New Order acolyte, calling him an *erlenmeyer* and ostracizing him from all their social activities.>

mingus (noun)
a social gathering or place notable for a lack of food, beverage, or other amenities <*usage instance:* One man's *mingus* is another man's citizenship-reaffirmation program.>

naysayer (noun)
one who opposes, denies, or is skeptical about something <*usage instance:* The wizards of the Old World claimed The One Who Is The One was a *naysayer,* until he *proved* their magic was empty trickery.>

pukka (or *pucka*) (adjective)
a. genuine b. first-class c. authentic to the age prior to the New Order Revolution <*usage instance:* Wiccans and other degenerates will often collect items they consider to be *pukka,* thereby lending valuable evidence to New Order police conducting home raids.>

straight and narrow (noun)
a. a person who always does things the same way, a bore b. *capitalized:* in myth and legend of the previous era, a person or animal incapable of traveling through a passageway to another universe or dimension of existence; cf. Curve[c] <*usage instance:* Since interdimensional portals do not exist, no one should ever feel slighted at being called a *Straight and Narrow.*>

314

Chapter 1

Whit

LISTEN TO ME. We don't have much time.

My name is Whit Allgood. I guess you've heard of me and my sister, Wisty, and of the crazy stuff that's happened, but here's the thing: *it's so much worse than you think it is.*

Trust me when I tell you that these are *the worst of times* and that the best of times are little more than a distant memory. And no one seems to be paying attention to what's going on. Are *you*?

Paying attention?

Imagine that all the things you love most in the world — and probably take for granted — are now *banned*. Your books, music, movies, art...all snatched away. Burned. That's life under the New Order, the so-called government — or brutal totalitarian regime — that's taken over this world. Now, with every waking breath, we have to fight for every freedom we have left. Even our *imagination* is at risk. Can you picture your government trying to destroy *that?* It's *inhuman.*

And yet... they're calling *us* criminals.

That's right. Wisty and I are the offenders in that unhappy propaganda piece brought to you by the New Order. Our crime? Engaging in free thought and creativity.... Oh, and practicing the "dark and foul arts" — i.e., magic.

Did I lose you? Let me back up a bit.

One night not so long ago, my family was awakened by soldiers storming through our home. Wisty and I were cruelly torn from our parents and slammed into a prison — a death camp for kids. And for what?

They accused us of being a witch and a wizard.

But, the thing is, it turns out the N.O. was actually right about that: we didn't know it at the time, but Wisty and I *do* have powers. *Magic* powers. And now we're scheduled to be publicly executed, along with our parents.

That particular ghoulish event hasn't taken place yet — though it will. I promise those of you who crave suspense, adventure, and bloodshed that you can look forward to it. And you *will,* if you're anything like the rest of the brainwashed "citizenry" of our land.

But if you're one of the few who've escaped the N.O.'s clutches, you *need* to hear my story. And Wisty's story. And the story of the Resistance. So when we're gone, there's someone left to spread the word.

Someone to fight the good fight.

And so we begin with the story of *another* public execution: a sad and unfortunate event, an accident, as luck or fate would have it. In a phrase that I hate to use under any circumstances: *a tragedy*.

Chapter 2

Whit

HERE'S WHAT HAPPENED, to the best of my shattered ability to recall it.

I do remember that I couldn't have been more lost and alone as I wandered the streets of this gray, crowded, and forsaken city. *Where is my sister? Where are the others from the Resistance?* I kept thinking, or maybe muttering the words like some homeless madman.

The New Order has already disfigured this once beautiful city beyond recognition. It seems like a decaying corpse swelling with mindless maggots. The suffocatingly low sky, the featureless buildings—even the faces of the nervously rushing people flooding around me—are as colorless and lifeless as the concrete under my feet.

I know the general populace has been efficiently brainwashed by the New Order, but these citizens seem a little *too* hushed, a little *too* urgent, a little *too* riveted to the scraps of propaganda clutched in their hands like prayer books.

Suddenly, my eyes spot a word in bold letters on the paper: EXECUTION.

And then the huge video displays hanging above the boulevard light up, and everything becomes clear to me. Every pedestrian stops and stands stock-still, and every head turns upward as if there has suddenly been an eclipse.

On the video screens, a hooded prisoner—small-framed, frail-looking—is kneeling on a starkly lit stage.

"Wisteria Allgood," blares a bone-chilling voice, "do you wish to confess to the use of the dark arts for the wicked purpose of undermining all that is good and proper in our society?"

This can't be happening. My heart is a big lump in my throat. *Wisty?* Did that voice really just say *Wisteria Allgood?* My sister's on an executioner's scaffold?

I grab a slack-jawed adult by his dismally gray overcoat lapels. "Where is this execution happening? Tell me right now!"

"The Courtyard of Justice." He blinks at me irritably, as if I've woken him from a deep sleep. "Where else?"

"Courtyard of Justice? Where's *that?*" I demand of the man, throwing my hands around his neck, nearly losing control of my own strength. I swear, I'm ready to throw this adult against a wall if I have to.

"Under the victory arch—down there," he gasps. He points at a boulevard that runs off to my left. "Let me go! I'll call the police!"

I shove him and take off running toward a massive ceremonial arch maybe a half mile away.

"You! Wait!" he yells after me. *"Don't I know your face from somewhere?"*

He does. Oh yes. And so would everyone else, if they took the time to notice that there was a wanted criminal running loose in their midst.

But his fellow citizens' eyes remain glued to the screen. They've got an insatiable appetite for malicious gossip of any kind and, of course, an equal taste for senseless death and destruction.

Even when the falsely condemned are kids. Just kids.

I can hear a distant roar now. The sound of hunger— for "justice," for blood.

I forge ahead into the pathetic herd of lemmings. *I'm not going to let them take my sister from me.* Not without a fight to the death anyway.

I round a corner, and then, across the top of the crowd, I see . . . *Is that my sister, Wisty, up on the stage?* She's hooded, dressed all in black, but standing now. Proudly. Brave as ever.

A man—if you would call him that—is on the stage with her. He's leaning on a crooked stick, his wickedly sharp black suit hanging strangely motionless in the wind that's begun to howl through the civic square. His angular face is glowing with smug self-satisfaction, as if he's just devoured a potful of whipping cream.

I know him; I despise him. *The One Who Is The One.* Quite possibly the most evil individual in the history of humanity.

Are there minutes or seconds left before this hideous execution? I have no way of knowing.

I knock people aside as I barrel through the thickening, or should I say *sickening*, throng. I can see a line of well-armed soldiers holding everyone back from the platform. If I can knock one of them down and snatch away a gun...

I look up at the stage just in time to see The One raise his knobby black stick and shake it menacingly at my sister. He has a look of absolute triumph.

"No!" I yell, but I'm unheard in the roaring crowd. They all know what's about to happen. I know, too. I just don't see how I can possibly stop it. There has to be a way.

"Nooo!" I scream. *"You can't do this! This is cold-blooded murder!"*

There's a flash—not of light but somehow of *blackness*—and she's gone. Wisty. My sister. My best friend in the world.

My little sister is dead.

THE GIFT – OUT NOW!

WITCH & WIZARD MOVIE NEWS!
Witch & Wizard is coming to theatres soon.
Read on for a sneak peek at the first scene.

READER NOTE:

THIS IS THE FIRST MOVIE IN THE SERIES BASED ON THE
#1 BESTSELLING BOOKS. WITCH & WIZARD TAKES PLACE IN
A MADE-UP WORLD, BUT THE LOOK OF THE MAIN CITY ISN'T
UNLIKE A LARGE CAPITAL IN THE U.S. OR EUROPE (AN
AMALGAM OF LONDON, BERLIN, DETROIT) — THEREFORE, THE
BUILDINGS, STREETS, THE OPEN AIR PRISON, ETC. CAN BE
DRESSED RATHER THAN CREATED FROM SCRATCH. THE
DIALOGUE IN THE SCRIPT IS STYLIZED: DRAMATIC,
SLIGHTLY THEATRICAL.

JAMES PATTERSON

A LAND NOT UNLIKE OUR OWN TROUBLED AND MISGUIDED ONE.
20 YEARS BEFORE THE RISE OF THE NEW ORDER.

EXT. ROAD - DAY

Stylized film. Beautiful. Painterly. A TEENAGE BOY, all
in black, pedals an ancient black bike toward a
stunningly handsome prep school: Purdy Day. The grounds
are gorgeous, rolling hills of green with stately
trees. The squeaking of the old bike breaks the
silence. Teenage Boy and his bike don't belong here.

INT. SCHOOL HALLWAY - DAY

The physically attractive, quiet TEENAGE BOY strides
down a noisy, crowded hallway of the blue-blood school.
He carries a thick sheaf of papers. He's wearing a long
black coat, jeans and very dusty engineer's boots.

He passes a knot of students in trademark preppy attire
(plaid skirts, blazers).

One of the students purposely bumps the Teenage Boy.

                    STUDENT 1
          Deliveries are through the back,
          friend.

                    STUDENT 2
          Hey, freakshow. Nice boots.

The students snigger and the Teenage Boy offers a
chilly smile and nod.

He strides past, turns a corner, and approaches a
secretary at a desk in front of the Headmaster's
Office.

                    TEENAGE BOY
          I need to see the Headmaster.

                    SECRETARY
          Do you have an appointment?

                    TEENAGE BOY
          No.

Teenage Boy continues past her desk. He's on a mission.

                    SECRETARY
        (indignant, picking up her phone)
        What do you think you're doing-!?

                    TEENAGE BOY
        I told you.

He turns the large bronze handle and forces open the
paneled door, stepping into the room beyond.

CLOSE ON - HIS HAND AS HE LOCKS THE DOOR BEHIND HIM.

INT. HEADMASTER'S OFFICE - DAY

The Headmaster, elitist, superior, uppity, and obnoxious
as hell, looks up in surprise and irritation at the
intruding boy.

                    HEADMASTER
        (with quintessential W.A.S.P. lockjaw)
        What? Really now. Who are you? You
        can't just-

The Teenage Boy drops smudged, wrinkled application
papers on the Headmaster's desk.

                    TEENAGE BOY
        Sir. I belong here at Purdy. Look at my
        work in public school. Perfect average.
        All-school academic awards-

                    HEADMASTER
        (standing up, waving him silent)
        Not another word. Not. One. Word. Who do
        you think you are? You don't fit in with
        our boys and girls. In fact, I'm hard
        pressed to think of a reputable school
        where you would fit in. Now go. Leave.

                    TEENAGE BOY
        I'm not finished.

                    HEADMASTER
        (nasty)
        Oh but you are! There is no way you will
        ever be admitted to Purdy Day. You are
        not like our students. You're common.
        Now remove your sadly confused self from
        my office, from this building, and from
        this campus.

INT. SECRETARY'S AREA - DAY

Two security guards arrive outside the Headmaster's
door. It's very tense. Anxious students and the
secretary gather behind the men.

                    HEAD OF SECURITY
              Sir? Headmaster! Is everything all
              right in there? Sir?
              The guards start to bang loudly on the
              door.

INT. HEADMASTER'S OFFICE - DAY

The Teenage Boy glares at the Headmaster with ax-murderer
intensity.

                    TEENAGE BOY
              I'll go. But let me show you something
              interesting first.

Teenage Boy shoots out both his hands at the
Headmaster.

What happens next is as stunning as it is unexpected.
The headmaster slowly begins to collapse in the manner
of a skyscraper being demolished by internal explosives.
All that's left of him is a small pile of ash on the
hardwood floor.

Teenage Boy throws open a window. The Headmaster's
ashes blow away.

                    TEENAGE BOY (CONT'D)
              (disdainful)
              You're right, I'm not like the other
              boys and girls here.

He slips out the open window, dropping two floors to
the lawn below.

EXT. ROAD - DAY

Teenage Boy leaves the handsome school grounds on his
old bike. He pedals faster and faster. Squeaking gets
louder and louder. He turns his head sharply. Off in
the distance, the school crumples to dust — much as the
headmaster did. Then Teenage Boy and bike vanish into
thin air.

                                   CUT TO BLACK:

FANG
A MAXIMUM RIDE NOVEL

James Patterson

FANG WILL BE THE FIRST TO DIE

Maximum Ride is used to surviving – living constantly under threat from evil forces sabotaging her quest to save the world – but nothing has ever come as close to destroying her as this horrifying prophecy. Fang is Max's best friend, her soulmate, her partner in leadership of her flock of bird kids. A life without Fang is a life unimaginable.

Max's desperate desire to protect Fang brings the two closer together than ever. But when a newly created winged boy, the magnificent Dylan, is introduced into the flock, their world is upended yet again. Raised in a lab like the others, Dylan exists for only one reason: he was created to be Max's perfect other half.

Thus unfolds a battle of science against soul, perfection versus passion, that terrifies, twists, and turns . . . and meanwhile, the apocalypse is coming.

OUT NOW!

DANIEL X:
DEMONS AND DRUIDS

James Patterson
& Adam Sadler

The Alien Hunter is playing with fire . . .

Daniel X is on an impossible mission: to eliminate every intergalactic criminal on the face of the Earth. Using his incredible superpower to create objects out of thin air, he's taken on some of the most fearsome and fiendish aliens in the universe. Now Daniel has travelled to England in search of his next target: the explosive demon of fire Phosphorius Beta and his army of flame-weaving henchmen.

But it's going to take a whole new level of mojo to destroy this villain. Beta's strength has been growing since he arrived on Earth more than a millennium ago, and he's finally ready to turn the blue planet into his own fiery wasteland. The only way to stop him is by jumping back in time to the Dark Ages to end Beta's blistering reign before it has a chance to begin. But can Daniel X take the heat? Or will the Alien Hunter finally get burned?

Join Daniel X on a wickedly wild ride – through space and time – for his most sizzling adventure yet!

A

I'm proud to be working with the National Literacy Trust, a great charity that wants to inspire a love of reading.

If you loved this book, don't keep it to yourself. Recommend it to a friend or family member who might enjoy it too. Sharing reading together can be more rewarding than just doing it alone, and is a great way to help other people to read.

Reading is a great way to let your imagination run riot – picking up a book gives you the chance to escape to a whole new world and make of it what you wish. If you're not sure what else to read, start with the things you love. Whether that's bikes, spies, animals, bugs, football, aliens or anything else besides. There'll always be something out there for you.

Could you inspire others to get reading? If so, then you might make a great Reading Champion. Reading Champions is a reading scheme run by the National Literacy Trust. Ask your school to sign up today by visiting www.readingchampions.org.uk.

Happy Reading!

James Patterson